SUPERWORSE:
THE NOVEL

SUPERWORSE: THE NOVEL

A Remix of *Superbad: Stories and Pieces* by
BEN GREENMAN

With a Foreword, a Midword, and
an Afterword by Laurence Onge
Edited by Laurence Onge

Soft Skull Press
Brooklyn, NY • 2004

Superworse: A Novel

© 2004 Ben Greenman

Book Design: David Janik
Editorial: Sarah Groff-Palermo
Cover photo: Kim Weston Photography | www.kimweston.com

Published by Soft Skull Press
71 Bond Street, Brooklyn, NY 11217

Distributed by Publishers Group West
1.800.788.3123 | www.pgw.com

Printed in Canada

Library of Congress Cataloging-in-Publication Data

Greenman, Ben.
Superworse : the novel : a remix of Superbad : stories and pieces /
by Ben Greenman ; with a foreword, a midword and an afterword
by Laurence Onge; edited by Laurence Onge.
    p. cm.
ISBN 1-932360-13-1 (pbk.: alk. paper)
I. Onge, Laurence. II. Title.
PS3607.R463 S87 2004
813'.6—dc22
                                        2003024148

TABLE OF CONTENTS

FOREWORD
By Laurence Onge

Some years ago, a former student of mine contacted me by telephone and asked me for a favor. Would I, he wanted to know, consider assisting him with the assembly and editing of a book of fiction? He had written a series of stories, you see, but he didn't trust himself to select them, you see, or for that matter, you see, to operate skillfully upon those he had selected. He said "you see" much too much for my tastes. It was a mark of callow-ness, which I would have been wise to have judged more harshly.

That student was Ben Greenman, who was a pupil of mine in graduate school many years ago. Prior to the phone call, if you had asked me for my recollections of Mr. Greenman, I would have given you a somewhat vague response: that he was industrious, that he sometimes asked probing questions, that he on occasion displayed a special kinship with the literary materials we were investigating. The truth would have been that this was a lie. Prior to the phone call, I didn't remember Ben Greenman any more clearly than I remembered Alan Smith, or Susan Rosenberg, or Zuza Glowacka, or any of the other students I have taught in the past decades. He was unremarkable. Still, I agreed to help him with his book. It is not a habit of mine to refuse the entreaties of my former students, especially when they express in no uncertain terms that they would never have written a word were it not for my inspirational example. ("Inspirational" was his word, not mine; I would never presume that I had a religious effect on a young mind.)

Superbad, *the book that resulted from that collaboration, was published by McSweeney's, a Brooklyn independent press, in 2001. Mr. Greenman contributed most of the writings: some two dozen short stories and pieces, some humorous, some serious, some musical. What he did not contribute—what he could not contribute—was a sense of order, a presiding intelligence. That was left to me. It is not too much of an exaggeration to say that without my intervention, the book would have been a welter of unresolved ideas, less a carefully assembled mosaic and more a gallimaufry of brightly colored tiles thrown together without regard for reason or rhyme. For starters, I was of the opinion that Mr. Greenman's finest work—a series of celebrity-themed musicals that dealt with such luminaries as Bill Gates, Bob Dylan, and Elian Gonzalez—was being undervalued. In the original manuscript, in fact, the musicals were treated as second-class citizens, and placed between "proper" stories like vaudeville interstitials. This was a shame, but the book succeeded nonetheless.*

Then it came time for the paperback reissue of Superbad, *the second budding of this peculiar flower. Mr. Greenman had announced to his paperback publisher—Soft Skull, yet another Brooklyn independent—that he planned to freshen the work by removing certain pieces and adding in others (including, most notably, "Sometree/Anytree," a botanical love story that has converted many readers, principally those of the distaff persuasion, to his oeuvre). The book would also be retitled: rather than* Superbad, *it would be called* Superworse. *When Soft Skull contacted me to see if I would serve as editor, I said that I would do it, but under one condition: that I had the freedom to comment upon the work at great length. Mr. Greenman is a talent. There is no doubt about that. But he is also a puzzle, and an obstacle, and a source of great remorse for me, and I wish for there to be no doubt about that either. If I was to unmuddy the water, I said, I would need to be in charge of all dams and locks.*

Soft Skull replied with a one-word telegram on classic Western Union onionskin: "Why?"

Why? Because this is a very complex book with an immense-

ly sophisticated architecture. During the assembly and editing of the hardback, I tried to convince Mr. Greenman to make his intentions transparent to readers. "An explanation of its central operating principle is necessary for the survival of this book," I wrote, "just as a trough of water is necessary for the survival of a horse. Without it, the horse of this book will grow parched, and possibly drink poisonous liquid desperately and die." I was poking fun at what I took to be his sometimes unpruned metaphors—more on that later—but my japery fell on deaf ears, as Mr. Greenman, like so many young artists, was more interested in the fashion of intrigue and mystery than in the fact of comprehension. His wife, whose name I can never remember (I believe that it starts with a consonant and ends with another consonant, though I concede that a vowel is also a possibility, in either station), wrote me a note that said as much: "Ben," it said, "knows that some readers will 'get him' and others will not, and he accepts both kinds of experience." I balked at this quite disgusting spectacle of relativism; the picture it conjured up was one of Mr. Greenman sitting aside a mountain peak, bodhisattva-like, cosseted in his enlightenment as the twin streams of truth and error flowed by on either side of him. I was also nonplussed by the use of the idiom "get him." All in all, it was too much to bear, and I promptly phoned Mr. Greenman and unleashed a torrent of abuse, using what I am sure was quite unforgivable language. But Mr. Greenman stood firm. He refused to heed my editorial imperatives. He was, poor boy, if not unaware of the nature of his own gift, at the very least uninterested in allowing it to reach others intact.

I remember those days well, when Mr. Greenman insisted upon his literary independence at the expense of his literature. They lasted through the publication of the hardback, Superbad, and I believe in my heart that they damaged the book's reception. If I had had the counsel of an older man in my early youth, who knows how much sooner I would have found my way to my life's work? Instead I had a father who ignored me but for scowling at me and spent most of his time playing the dogs. As it transpired,

I did not suffer in his presence long, although it was much too long for my tastes. At seventeen, I left Toronto for Chicago, convinced that I would never return, and under my arm I carried a briefcase filled with a tattered copy of Paradise Lost, *a somewhat dejected fedora, and a letter informing me that a spot was being reserved for me in a university whose name, even today, is like a song upon my lips. From that point on, I had several mentors, each more prominent than the next. With their help, I reached my present altitude; without them, it is entirely possible I would have remained earthbound, or sunk even lower.*

So I have had it bad and I have had it good, to quote from the old song, but I have always had it. Mr. Greenman did not have it, because he would not have it. After the hardback, however, I was more determined than ever to help him place his work at the proper focal distance from readers, so that it would be sharply seen, and sharply experienced. That is when Soft Skull permitted me to go to work overseeing this paperback. The problems were not few. For starters, Mr. Greenman has an unfortunate habit of writing too quickly. The words come out of him like exhaust from an automobile, and if the vehicle eventually reaches its destination, the exhaust has by then dissipated. (Above, I reprinted a quite unforgivable metaphor about a horse drinking water. This was satire and even parody; Mr. Greenman once wrote me a postcard that insisted, somewhat flippantly, that "a metaphor should take no longer to develop than a Polaroid." That is haste and waste and folly; this automotive metaphor took me two solid hours to compose, including the time spent drawing diagrams of cars, exhaust, and prevailing winds.) Also, Mr. Greenman wishes to be too many things at once, in the fashion of a hippogriff: the first iteration of Superbad, *the hardback, was praised with a squib from the wonderful novelist Susan Minot: "I don't know what goes on in Ben Greenman's mind, but inside it there seems to be a Russian short story writer, a slapstick gag writer, an art critic, a literary critic, a cultural commentator, a cowboy, a satirist, a scientist, a postmodernist, an antipostmodernist, a surrealist, a nut, a genius, a stand-up comedian, a child prodigy, a dreamer, and a poet." Is this not the very definition of a crazy man?*

A lesser editor, or a less devoted mentor, would have left Mr. Greenman bobbing in the rapids of his writing and the whirlpool of his multifarious identities, and it is likely that he would have drowned. I did not. I could not. The paperback, I knew, would need a strong hand to guide it, and I was just the hand. Working closely with Soft Skull's editorial board, I devised a solution. In addition to penning a foreword and an afterword, and appending modest comments to the head of a number of individual pieces (albeit a small number: I believed, and believe, in limiting intervention; the magician does not step into the audience and shove his hands into pockets), I would write a midword. By the time a reader finished with Superworse, *the* Superworse *that I had helped to ripen, he or she would taste the full flavor of Mr. Greenman's talent—would understand, in short, why this collection of pieces is not merely an opportunistic assembly but an intricately constructed novel. I took leave from the university and bought a small sports car. I drove the car to New York City and rented a small apartment. I sat in the apartment at a small desk and made notes on a small piece of paper with a small pencil. The results, ironically, were monumental. The inner workings of the book are illuminated, like a watch broken open and set beneath a blazing lamp. Skeptics cluck their tongues. That's what they do. They seem to have tongues that cluck continuously. They want to know if my role has been overdetermined by earlier literature, both prescribed and foreclosed. They want to know whether I can step out of the shade of* Pale Fire, *erase memories of Virgil's interventions in the* Inferno, *or eclipse the assistance Pound offered Eliot in the composition of* The Waste Land. *I can answer that with two words: I cannot. I can only commit the crime of improvement. To the charge of "il miglior fabbro" I plead guilty.*

I. ILL IN '99

I was ill in '99. I got better from the turn of the century on—
something about the weather, or my wife, or the hopeful way
people looked at me in the street. But by 2011 I was dying again,
and there was nothing that anyone could do about it.

Sky hours measure how long you've been around. I remember
them from my childhood. There were only sky hours then—sky
hours in the crystal fifties, the brilliant sixties, the broad seventies. Stone hours measure how long you have left. After '99, I
had mostly stone hours. I wasn't an old man when the illness first
came on. I had some youth still. But I had less than I imagined.

I was sick at the same time as Merv Griffin, the famous talk-
show host and game-show tycoon who was later elected to the
U.S. Senate. Merv was much older than me, but some mornings
I felt as old as Merv. This was a result of the illness, certainly, and
by that I mean my illness and not Merv's. Merv had cancer, which
eats you slowly. I had something much hungrier.

In the restless nineties I worked in construction, a real muscle-
man profession. I carried iron beams from place to place, lugged
bales of welding wire, fastened flat countersunk head rivets. Some
days I worked without a hard hat. That's how tough a customer I
was. By 2005, I was long off the sites, bumped up to the execu-
tive tier, so it only made sense for me to quit the construction
racket and move on to be the nation's secretary of publicity. I
headed up the Department of How Things Are, which was located in a menacing, ash black building right across the street from

1

the petite, pink offices of the Department of How Things Should Be. My job mostly involved circling pictures of women's breasts in fashion magazines. It wasn't the easiest job in the world—I had to use one of those permanent markers, and the squeaking and the smell damned near drove me nuts some days—but I got really good at it, and by my third month there I rarely accidentally circled the head or the hand.

Castelloni and Davies were my right-hand men.

Castelloni was an actor. When I was a kid he was the star of a TV show called *Russell Aikens*, as Russell Aikens, who was a kind of superhero. His slogan was "Geography Teacher by Day, Crimefighter by Night." That slogan became a euphemism for gay people and the double life they led. If my friends and I saw a particularly swishy guy out on the street, we'd elbow one another in the chest. "Geography teacher by day, crimefighter by night," we'd snicker, and eventually we just shortened it to "geography teacher by day." Castelloni wasn't gay. He was a mean bastard who was closer in character to the assassins and mob bosses that he went on to play in the movies. He would call you what he wanted to call you and hit you when you were down. Once we were debating how to tell the nation about drilling on Utah's Kaiparowits Plateau. "We should just tell them," Castelloni said. His thick face was a terrible red. "Tell them where we're going to drill, and if they don't like it, we'll just drill a hole into their fucking skulls with one of those cordless drills! If we can't do the job, maybe we should farm it out to those pansy-ass pinheads at the Department of How Things Should Be." At the end of his rather persuasive speech, he was screaming so loud that he clutched his jaw as if he had dislocated it.

Davies was a geography teacher by day.

We worked as a crack team, the three of us. Or rather, they worked and I supervised. The breast-circling kept me busy most of the day, and at night I would go home and eat a simple meal off of one of the commemorative plates my ex-wife and I had collected: the Space Shuttle plate, the Berlin Wall dismantling plate, or the Canadian Unpleasantness plate. Then I'd watch some TV, go to sleep, and wake up early enough to be back in the office by 8 A.M. As a result, I only had a few minutes each day to design the nation's intellectual and moral agenda and write up press releases that would advance that agenda. But what a glorious few minutes! One day I wrote this release, which went out along the wires in time to make the evening news:

> Our Good Citizens: Great leaders from our past, like Roosevelt, Wilson, and Johnson, rose to the tops of nations that required their leadership. But the Americas of Roosevelt, Wilson, and Johnson no longer exist; they are not the America we see today. Roosevelt, Wilson, and Johnson spent their lives wrestling with issues vital to the nation's survival—with industrialization, with aggression from overseas, with an internal inequity that threatened to erupt into a sort of cultural civil war. Today these are not concerns. The problems of our time are more difficult. They are not about technological progress. We have more technological progress than we know how to handle. They are not about peacetime and wartime. The difference between those two states disappeared a long time ago. They are not about race. All races are equalized, if not always equal. Now, as we look toward the middle of this new century, we must disenthrall ourselves with the concerns of the past and confront the issues of the present, which will become the issues of the future. I will now list those issues. Goodbye, and goodnight.

It was a version of a speech by John Kennedy, right down to the word *disenthrall*, but with one important difference. My release had no point. I had the buildup in place. I had all of America waiting for the issues. But then—no bang. No pitch. No nothing.

This was part of the plan.

In the time before the establishment of the Department, the entire nation—the men in suits, the women in skirts, the children who attested to the willingness of those men and women to couple with one another, if not always to connect—watched the government with an indifference that canted more toward contempt than resentment. They felt superior to their caretakers, above those who labored to give them a better life. They weren't afraid of government. They simply felt that it didn't serve their needs. This was shortly after the nineties drew to a close. As a result of this contempt for government, many television and film celebrities from the broad seventies were elected to government—not just Merv Griffin, who to date has served four terms in the U.S. Senate, but Representatives Clint Eastwood, Dustin Hoffman, Mike Douglas, and Faye Dunaway. Contrary to the myth perpetuated by some of our less reputable historians, popular movie star Robert Redford did not pursue a career in politics, although there was a one-term Representative from Utah named Robert Redword who was also a Kleagle in the Salt Lake City Ku Klux Klan. At any rate, the formation of the Department of How Things Are galvanized the public, satisfying the clumsy, childlike need to be organized that had gone unaddressed during the broad seventies, the booming eighties, and the restless nineties. In its early years, the Department offered a sanctuary from the terrors of a chaotic world, sending out recommendation memos that instructed "Our Good Citizens" (for this was how we addressed them, always, as a form of positive reinforcement) what they should watch on television, which magazines they should read, in what order they should go through the sections of the morning newspaper (sports first, then news, then business news, then entertainment). Department officials encouraged people to turn in their neighbors when they discovered them violating the recommendations.

In the second half-decade of operation, though, the Department's philosophy shifted. I was primarily responsible for the shift, having arrived from the world of construction with a bee in my bonnet about reforming the government's propaganda operation. The first weekend of my administration, I scheduled a retreat with my top managers—Castelloni, Davies, and a third man who had the strange name of Weaver Cinnamon. Weaver Cinnamon was the youngest of us all, no more than thirty when he joined the Department in 2005. He was from a tiny Arkansas town named Subiaco, where the Cinnamon family owned a neighborhood grocery. He had risen through the ranks quickly, in part because he was a quick study, in part because he had a good personality, and in part because he was the most handsome man anyone had ever seen, with a strong jawline, steel gray eyes, and perfect, rugged features that looked as if they had been sculpted with God's own chisel. Weaver Cinnamon was hard to look at, he was so handsome, but he was easy to promote.

We took our retreat on the northeast coast of Canada, which was still a friendly nation then, and on the second afternoon there Weaver Cinnamon went hiking by himself. He made it all the way up a small mountain near the camp, arriving just at sunset, and then stood there, silhouetted by the red sky, the shelf of the ridge jutting out beneath him. Off in the distance, a sailboat was in irons in the water, and from where we stood, on the lower plateau, it looked as if the sailors, too, were watching Weaver Cinnamon as he stood atop the ridge. "Isn't he beautiful?" said Davies.

"Shut up!" snapped Castelloni, but without his usual ire. Even Castelloni liked Weaver Cinammon.

The next morning, after listening to a radio address by Senator Griffin that condemned a recent string of church burnings in the New Southwest—Merv was still going strong then, not yet cancer-ridden—I called the group together, only to find that Weaver Cinnamon was nowhere to be found. Neither Castelloni nor Davies had seen him since we had all seen him standing on the mountain. We knew better than to mess with the Canadian wild ourselves, so we called the Mounties quickly, and in about ten hours, they brought back the chewed corpse of Weaver Cinnamon. "Killer wolves," the Mountie captain said. "Maybe bears." He wasn't so bad-looking himself, this Mountie captain, but he was nothing like Weaver Cinnamon. We buried Cinnamon the next day in a small cemetery whose other residents all seemed to be members of the same family, and the day after that, back in Washington, my two top lieutenants and I, all three of us still tearful from the loss of our youngest and handsomest colleague, sat down to map out our plan for the Department. That's how we came to be the most powerful part of the government—more powerful than the Department of the Interior, more powerful than the Department of Defense, more powerful than the Fed or the president. We were impelled forward by grief.

The decade dragged on. We dodged boredom. I can't go into the details of our activities—they are all classified—but suffice it to say that we destroyed a few major religions, commissioned the occasional assassination, and circled more than two hundred thousand pairs of breasts between January 1, 2006, and December 1, 2010. The figures for this year haven't yet been tabulated. We also released a steady stream of speeches and statements that kept America numb and kept Americans guessing. What was the government thinking? What was the government doing? We weren't telling. Then last Wednesday, Castelloni came up to me. He was screaming, as always. "Moron!" he said. "Go to the doctor! Idiot!" The advice came out of nowhere—since '99, I had been the picture of health, with only an occasional onset of flu-like symptoms or floaters in my field of vision, which I attributed to too much television. Other than that, I hadn't had so much as a nosebleed. But if Castelloni noticed something, I was willing to consider the possibility. He was always a very perceptive man. Davies visited me in my office later, and sat on my desk and nervously pinched the pleats of his pants. "Chief," he said. "You seem awful. Your circles around these breasts are irregularly shaped, and sometimes you're Xing them instead of circling them. Plus, you look haggard and drawn, and at least twenty years older than you are." Then he started telling me about how his new lover's parents hadn't really accepted him yet. I went down to give some blood, in part so that the doctors could determine how sick I was and in part to escape Davies's endless confession. He did that kind of thing—oh they won't accept me, oh my life's so hard—about twice a week. It got old fast. The med staff made me wait for about an hour, and then the nurse ushered me in. She was tall and had reddish hair, and she kept palpating my stomach and asking me how it felt.

While I waited for the results of my tests, I told the nurse about how just days before I had convinced a libertarian governor of a traditionally Republican state to sign a bill that required criminals convicted of multiple crimes to be sentenced under whichever offense carried the highest penalty. The nurse was impressed. She was a politics buff, she said, and had always had difficulty finding other people to talk to about the pressing issues of our time.

"I can imagine," I said. What I didn't say is that not only could I imagine the nation's apathy, but that I had induced the nation's apathy. It was part of the plan. Each day, Castelloni, Davies, and I set out to strip Americans of what little of their political interest remained. That was why we released so many confusing and nonsensical statements. And we had, for the most part, succeeded. Still fawning over me—I guess it's not every day that the secretary of publicity drops by for a checkup—the nurse asked me out for a drink, and off we went. The two of us got really sloshed on boilermakers, and before I knew it she was talking about Jimmy Carter, who was president at the end of the broad seventies. "He was such a good man," she said, "and so maligned for no good reason."

"I don't know," I said. "I'm somewhat partial to Ted Kennedy."

She wrinkled up her nose. "I just know him because he ran against Carter in the 1980 primaries," she said. "Wasn't he a drunk?"

"Probably," I said. "His wife Joan was. And Ted had his problems with the bottle, too, not to mention some difficulty with fidelity. I didn't see it, you know. I heard things. But despite those flaws, he was a great leader. He lived through the assassinations of both his brothers—John, who was president in the brilliant sixties, and Robert, who ran for president. And he kept his influence in the Senate right through to his death."

"But Carter," she said, "restored morality to the nation. And despite soaring energy costs and a really problematic economy, not to mention tensions in the Middle East, he stabilized the country. Plus, after his presidency, he kept helping people. I think he's one of the most important figures of the last forty years. He's right up there with Mike Douglas."

"Look," I said, "this is a silly conversation. Both Carter and

Kennedy are long gone. What are we fighting about here? And why would you even mention someone like Mike Douglas? Douglas isn't even as important as Dick Cavett, and neither of them can really compare with Merv Griffin. Who negotiated a disengagement agreement with Honduras and Mexico? Who pushed through funding for the first residential space station? Who co-authored the Griffin-Jarvis Bill, which regulated privatized education? I mean, Griffin gets cancer, and still he's volunteering for more committee assignments."

"Well," she said, and then she said "well" again. She sounded angry. "By the way, I got your test results. You're dying."

"Hey," I said, somewhat taken aback. "If you don't want to talk about politics, that's fine with me. We could talk about movies."

"No," she said. "You're really dying. It might take a week, maybe a month. But you're about to be dead."

When I got home that night I collapsed on the couch and thought about death. I thought about Weaver Cinnamon, and how ugly and diminished his beautiful face had looked half-eaten by wolves, or bears, or whatever they were. Then I went to the digital phone book and tried in vain to find my ex-wife's number. Her name was Lisa and she was an American Indian. Lisa isn't a name often associated with American Indians, but Lisa looked like Cher, who was a famous singer at around the same time Merv Griffin was a famous talk-show host, and was also the co-host of her very own variety show along with her husband Sonny Bono, a short singer who was later in government, though not with a position as important as mine or Merv Griffin's.

Lisa taught me many things about the spirit. That's the wonderful thing about American Indians. They are people of the spirit. They trap rabbits with their bare hands and use every part of the animal—the meat, the pelt, the teeth. They extract the rabbit's eyes and use them for native medicine, and the myelin that coats the rabbit's muscles is chemically altered in their factories and resold as a powerful industrial lubricant. But what they do to rabbits is only the beginning. These people build a bridge between the vast plains and the vast sky. In their mind, I mean. A bridge in their mind. With the materials of their spirits.

Lisa's hair was jet black, much darker than mine. One night in '99, in the time of my first illness, my hair turned white. Snow-white, to be precise. And it did actually happen overnight. I went to bed with my hair as brown as shoe leather, and woke with it as white as snow. I'm not sure how this happened, but it parallels the case of Bob Barker, who was a game-show host at the same time that Senator Merv Griffin had his talk show and Cher had her variety show. Those were the broad seventies, which represented the peak of talk shows until the restless nineties. In the nineties, even Clifton Chenier, who was an accordion player who specialized in a New Orleans music called zydeco, had his own morning talk show. In fact, Lisa was watching *Bonjour Chenier* the morning I woke up with my snow white hair.

That was in '99, and we were young marrieds in the tender zone of early bliss. That's when we started to collect the commemorative plates. We collected the plates as if our love would last forever. It lasted somewhat less than forever—six years to be exact—and when it ended, Lisa smashed up the plate that depicted the public funeral of Don Henley, who was a popular singer before he was elected governor of California and then martyred by an assassin's bullet. Then it was ought-eleven, and I was moving like a melody toward my final reward, and that's when I decided to call Lisa and set things right with her once and for all. The only problem was, I didn't know where to find her. Lisa had been a waitress and a bartender when she was my wife. When we split up, she went to work in a figurine factory. She was doing her part to help along the American Manufacturing Renaissance. She was gluing the huge plastic heads onto the tiny plastic bodies of Nancy Reagan dolls.

Soon after I learned I would die, I remembered what Lisa taught me about sky hours and stone hours. And soon after that, I went by the bar where she used to work and slapped the backs of the drunks who introduced us, who saw that we would be perfect for one another and build a house of perfect love in the sky.

Tom Lehman was the oldest drunk there, about the same age as Senator Eastwood, and he was also one of my oldest friends. "Come outside with me, Tom," I said.

Outside, Tom and I sat on a bench. We talked about his ex-wife, and his kids, and his ailing mother, and then we talked about the recent wave of nostalgia for the broad séventies. "That Merv Griffin," said Tom Lehman. "Do you think he is a geography teacher by day?"

"Maybe," I said. "But he's a great man, Tom." There was a lump in my throat. I couldn't help it. Thinking about Merv always got me choked up that way.

We talked more about the movies, and sports, and work. "How's the tit-circling biz?" Tom said. I said it was fine. I asked Tom if he had heard from Lisa. Tom looked at me long and hard. "You don't know?"

"I guess not," I said.

"She's dead," he said. "We all got cards about it from her mother. There was an accident at the factory. I'm sorry. I thought for sure you'd know." We sat together. A television somewhere in the distance was playing a rerun of some talk show from the booming eighties. Tom Lehman struggled to his feet, took a whiz, zipped up haphazardly, shook my shaking hand with his wet hand, and went. I didn't get a chance to tell him I was dying.

By the urine water of Tom Lehman I sat down and wept. That's when I saw Lisa. She came back to me, appeared in the evening air behind the bar and hung there like a vision, her long black hair rippling with something more than ordinary energy. She didn't say anything, but she was smiling, and her smile came to me as a gift and not as a humiliation. I didn't need to watch the buffalo gallop away, which is a euphemism for being humiliated that is popular among the American Indians. Lisa looked like something I needed but could never have. She always looked that way. In her left hand, there was something circular and white; as I moved closer, I saw that it was a commemorative plate, with a picture of Merv Griffin and a simple inscription: "1925–2011: Served His Country Well." Merv looked great on the plate. He didn't look a day over seventy. He smiled, benign and wise, his silver hair shining like an altarpiece, and then the plate began to rise out of Lisa's hand. It rose until it was even with her head, and kept rising, until it was over her like a sun or a moon. Simple, floating, it was the last thing I saw.

II. Notes on Revising Last Night's Dream

Talking parrot needs to lose Ricky Ricardo accent.

Old girlfriend who has moved on to date other men should not look so beautiful.

Replace man wearing black hat (trite!) with woman wearing red shoes (cinematic!).

Tibet has no stock-car racing.

Knife next to breakfast plate need not bloom into flowers.

More invisibillity.

III. Snapshot

Editor's Note:

When he first sent me this chapter, about a year before the appearance of the hardback edition of *Superbad*, Mr. Greenman attached a note in which he wrote the following: "Trying new strategy. Having story translated into Russian by one undergraduate and then back into English by another." He called this double reflection *funhousing*, and it was impossible to tell from that note whether he was in earnest or not. In those days, I was not yet living in New York City, but rather visiting from Chicago, working on Mr. Greenman's book in the mornings and then taking long walks in the afternoon, which sometimes stretched from the West Village all the way up to Chelsea. I asked Mr. Greenman to meet and discuss this *funhousing*—if it was in fact the case, I wanted more details—and he agreed to meet me at a coffee shop in Times Square, where locals keep their heads down, noses in newspapers, and tourists shuffle in chain-gang formation from store to store. I saw a clutch of Russians wearing lots of red; it was in their visors and their sneakers and the shorts that they insist upon despite the weather. The men were beefy but not fat. The boys were miniature versions of their fathers and appalled enough by this development that they walked too far ahead before they were recalled with a shout; the fathers liked to shout at the sons and the sons didn't mind being shouted at; it was a way of making blood audible, or else it didn't mean anything at all. The wives seemed to exist mainly for the purpose of carrying cameras. "Fatagrafeeya," they said, which I knew from Mr. Greenman's story to be the Russian word for photograph. Mr. Greenman did not show up that day, and the funhousing matter was never settled, but I took the coincidence as a form of succor.

13

It is April. In Moscow the cherry blossoms are in bloom, and fleecy boughs canopy the flat gray streets. One morning, over his toast and coffee, Pyotor Petrovich reads of a dispute between American and British researchers played out in the pages of the *London Journal of Scientific Inquiry*. A distinguished British physicist has challenged the unorthodox results of an American team, insinuating that he is not satisfied with the soundness of their laboratory methods. Pyotor Petrovich is a conscientious man, and this sort of thing upsets him greatly. When he was a young graduate student, his mentor, the esteemed Dr. Alexsandr Rostikov, was infamous for the scornful gaze he would fix upon students remiss in their experimental preparations. Rostikov would tower over the helpless tyro, and then, from the Andean peak of his unimpeachable intelligence, issue a single scathing word: "Careless!" Pyotor Petrovich only needed one such incident to terrify him and to convince him of the absolute necessity of meticulous order, both within the scientist and in the environment around him. "We are caretakers of new realities," Pyotor Petrovich often explains to his younger colleagues, his rhetoric and delivery altogether less magisterial than Rostikov's, but every bit as heartfelt. "The experiment is a world, and its Genesis must be seamless. What happens afterward, we cannot say. We can only watch. The apple may be plucked and eaten. The apple may be left untouched. After the setup, we are a perfect eye. But during the setup, we are the one and only God." This deistic metaphor rarely finds favor among the younger researchers, who view it as a quaint myth of impossible exactitude, but even they agree that procedural prudence is vital.

Pyotor Petrovich's initial suspicions regarding the *London Journal* case, which arise during his breakfast, are only confirmed by his second reading, which takes place on the bus from his flat to Drudzgrad-7, the secret research city just south of the capital, and his third, which occurs while he is waiting to enter the I-9 Lab. The Britisher, it seems, is trying to return to prominence after nearly a decade of relative invisibility, and the upstart group of young researchers from Baltimore has had the misfortune of serving as the first victims of this renewed vigor. Not only because he tends to side with the underdogs—it is in Pyotor Petrovich's nature to support some notion of universal parity, where all benefits and deficits are subtly counterweighed—but because of the clear facts of the controversy, which he reviews as he eats his modest lunch of cheese and onion, that he finds himself growing increasingly incensed at what he perceives as unjust treatment of the Americans. In at least one section of his challenge, this Englishman has resorted to irresponsible conjecture regarding the execution of a Hungarian experiment of 1978, and this egregious misreading of the Rackozy setup invalidates his entire argument. Pyotor Petrovich hopes the Americans are aware of this flaw in the attack, but he has his doubts—few men in the world, he knows, are as attentive to these minute details of operations as he is. Greatly agitated, he paces his small office space, all the while ticking a fingernail across the rim of his styrofoam coffee cup, and then, in a quite uncharacteristic outburst, bangs a closed fist against the flat white formica of his lab table. "This is true injustice!" he exclaims loudly. Natalya Azkharava, the thick brunette in charge of equipment requisitioning, looks up from her desk and gazes quizzically through the glass partition. Pyotor Petrovich returns an abashed smile. But all afternoon, as he fits lenses and samples wavelengths, he cannot help thinking of the team of four Americans, and how they must be clustered around a conference table in the Johns Hopkins University, picking nervously at cold meats and vegetables as they draft and re-draft letters of protest. "We the undersigned wish to object strenuously to the charges of our distinguished colleague . . ." "It is with great certitude that we reassert our original results and urge the withdrawal of this unwarranted criticism . . . " "We appeal to the fairness and objectivity of the international community . . ."

From the top drawer of his desk, Pyotor Petrovich withdraws his prized fountain pen—he ordered it years before from a French catalog, and was overjoyed when it met and even exceeded the beauty of the model pictured in the advertisement—and writes to Dr. L. Rashman, the lead researcher on the American study. Pyotor Petrovich is very proud of his English, almost as proud as he is of his pen. He had spent some time in London as a student during the fifties, and attended a play starring Jean Simmons, something about a young boy imprisoned in a manor house by his beautiful but tyrannical aunt. After the play, he stood outside on Shaftesbury Avenue with the crowds, waiting for Simmons to emerge, and when she did, he extended his play-bill to her deferentially. He kept the program, the actress's name scrawled in two hurried tiers across its face, and when he returned from London presented it to his fiancée as a gift, along with a love note in fluent English. It is with that same English—weakened slightly, of course, by the intervening decades, but still more than adequate—that he writes to the American doctor in condolence and commiseration. "Doctor Rashman, I know how great must be your discomfort," he writes in a careful script, his lower lip folded inward with concentration. "I am research scientist here in Russia and an associate of the late Doctor Alexsandr Rostikov, with whom you are perhaps familiar. I studied under him years ago. In reading the *London Journal of Scientific Inquiry*, I have looked at an article about your research team what I feel is most unjust. Please send to me a copy of your original article. I would like to read of your work and then to write on your behalf to those who I know. Also, that you would read the 1978 paper delivered by G. Rackozy in Budapest, and that you would see the errors of Dr. Phillips in applying it to this case. I sense that you are in the right, and hope to help convince others of this." After signing his name, Pyotor Petrovich rereads the letter, and feeling that he has assumed a tone at once too condescending and too pessimistic, adds a light-hearted postscript: "I wish that you will accept my humble assistance, and hope that you are not a rash man."

After sealing the letter in a crisp envelope of a watery green color, Pyotor Petrovich deposits it in a red wire basket on the far right of his desk. The basket is situated just in front of a photograph of his wife, long dead, and his two sons, who are grown now and live nearby. Behind those photographs are more: another of his wife as a young bride, his sons playing in the snow, him and Anna on holiday. He has practiced this hobby of amateur photography for more than thirty years, and his persistence has rewarded him with countless photographs of his family and friends and none at all of himself. In the one photograph in which Pyotor Petrovich should appear, a lab snapshot that shows him working with Rostikov, his face is obscured by a beaker perched upon a ringstand. According to his own record, he is an ontological naught; he often jokes that if he were to vanish, it would be without a trace. And yet, a discerning eye would find evidence of him everywhere. In the careful maintenance of the lab's lasers; in the white coat, right cuff rubbed with ink, that hangs upon the corner hook; in the apple and the pastry missing from the Drudzgrad-7 commissary every afternoon. And even in the pictures themselves, in the way the faces of the subjects reach across the photographic plane and locate him with love.

The advancing spring is retreating dawn, and bringing the first few rays of light to the early morning hours. Pyotor Petrovich lives in a small flat that he has rented with prompt monthly payments for the nine years since his wife's death. A tiny corner kitchen, a sofa that folds out into a bed, and a large mahogany bookshelf. They are mostly his wife's books; she was a poet, and she collected other poets in thin brown volumes, Akhmatova, Tsvetaeva, Mandelstam. Each morning he rises at half-past five, washes down flavorless toast with lukewarm coffee, and then walks to the corner to catch the government bus into the research park. He is usually among the first to arrive at his building, and he awaits the opening of the Checkpoint Alexei security gate along with the other obsessively punctual chemists and botanists, astrophysicists and physicists. The men who gather in the early morning arrange themselves into informal fours and fives, and wonder aloud about the condition of the country, especially the rapid change that is occurring in the national rhetoric. Pyotor Petrovich himself has a set of stock comments, most of which are cut with the cautionary saws of folk tales; Gorbachev is both the prince and the fool, or change is a golden ball coveted by an avaricious empress. The aeronautics engineers who work the East Wing are the least agreeable to these impromptu conferences—a close-knit group of tall and haughty men susceptible to affectations, monocles and pocket-watch chains, they are not native Russians, but the sons of German exiles who came East as defectors in the wake of the Nazi downfall. Their labs reflect their otherness, and are arranged with forbidding Kopfvedreher precision, instruments tagged and sorted, circles chalked on the countertops to indicate the proper storage zones for instruments.

Pyotor Petrovich, by contrast, approaches his work as a natural extension of his life, continuous with his domestic existence, and as a result, his laboratory is decorated like the modest home of a cottager—like his own home, in fact. Lab equipment and scientific paperwork are juxtaposed haphazardly with chance articles of cheap furniture—a compact cubic refrigerator and a red velour easy chair, a weatherbeaten mahogany end-table, and a wall-mounted plywood shelf that holds volumes of Pushkin, Flaubert, and his beloved Dostoevsky. This shelf overhangs a small metal workbench at the rear of the lab, and it is Pyotor Petrovich's sanctum. For more than a decade now, he has been collecting castaway parts from neighboring labs and cobbling together inventions, experimenting with small advances in electronics and optical technology. The previous summer, for instance, he had begun work on a perfectly flat video monitor, thin as card stock, and he had recently drafted plans for a portrait camera equipped with an automatic framing feature. Almost none of these devices works correctly—the video monitor, for instance, can display only one image per second, rendering it insufficient for anything but novelty status—but this does not worry Pyotor Petrovich. In fact, it is the very failure of his inventions to function that engages him. Imperfect, incapable, unresolved, they inspire in him a sentiment that transcends pragmatic concerns; they are like children who will never grow up, and will always need the guiding hand of a parent to find their way in the world. The longer he spends tinkering with their circuits without definitive results, the more affection he feels for them. They need him.

It is an overcast day, threatening yet another May rain, when Pyotor Petrovich receives a manila envelope in the mail. It is three weeks after he has sent his letter to Johns Hopkins—he has been waiting eagerly for a response—and his heart thrills when he sees that the envelope is posted with an American stamp, a watercolor of the Wright Brothers at Kitty Hawk. Before he even opens the envelope, he razors off its post-corner; he must show this stamp to the aeronautics engineers. This is who they have to thank, not their Venckmanns and von Brauns. For a letter-opener, he uses a dull butter knife, sawing away at the flap until he finally extracts a neatly folded sheet of stationery. It is white but not white, and he holds it against the formica top to better gauge its color. Cream. The letter is from Dr. Rashman, and it is forthright and friendly, exactly as he imagines America:

> Dear Dr. Petrovich, I thank you very much for your interest in our case. I am happy to inform you that we have reached an understanding with Dr. Phillips, and that he has ceased to hint at improprieties. He has not yet apologized for casting aspersions, but as a colleague of mine has remarked, we're not holding our breath. Still, the last few weeks have been difficult, sometimes maddeningly so, and I cannot tell you how much I appreciate the support of colleagues across the globe. I was especially intrigued to learn of your association with Dr. Rostikov, whose work provided the foundation for so much of my own. We scientists work too often with theoretical propositions, isolated from phenomenal fact, and though I have seen countless photographs of the man, I never until now conceived of him as an actual corporeal being, someone with students and friends. If for nothing else, I thank you for helping to give a certain heft to my professional imaginations.

The final paragraph is short, but despite its brevity Pyotor Petrovich has to read it a few times to be certain that he has understood: *In response to your wonderful postscript, I must admit that I am not a rash man. In fact, I am not a man at all. Your, Dr. Lila Rashman.* A woman. He never would have guessed, and yet now that he knows he is not surprised.

The American has enclosed an article about the resolution of the conflict, the opposing parties making a public show of goodwill at an international conference held in New York City. Alongside the article, the journal has printed a photograph of the Hopkins team, all of them smiling broadly and one of them, a stout fiftyish woman, gripping the hand of the Englishman. Pyotor Petrovich searches the caption, and is relieved to learn that this is not Dr. Rashman. He finds her finally in the left foreground, standing behind a table. She is a tall woman with long black hair and a penetrating gaze, and she looks rather young, no older than thirty-five. A slight warmth rises into his face. The photograph does not flatter her entirely—there is something thick and rectangular about the set of her jaw—but this Pyotor Petrovich chalks up to the cruelty of the camera. He knows how it can falsify; his wife, slight and small, always looked slightly overweight in photographs, with an overbite his sympathetic gaze could not detect.

He mounts the photograph on the wall over his workbench. As the afternoon proceeds, he comes to understand it better. Some of the heaviness of her face results from the shadow cast by the figure to her left, a well-known Harvard mathematician whose name he cannot recall now. And while the woman is older than he initially suspected—at least forty, he now guesses—he can see her twentieth year in the playful tilt of her head, her tenth in the unguarded brilliance of her smile. But it is her eyes that draw him most powerfully, with such a luminosity that looking into them, even through the intervening medium of the photograph, is like listening to the voice of their owner. The magic of this photograph, and of photographs in general, lies in the multiplicity of their effect, the way they operate both viscerally and surreptitiously, simultaneously presenting a simulacrum of reality to the intellect and floating undetected into the recesses of the mind (memory, desire) like wisps of fragrance from a bakery window. Anyone could look at this picture and fall in love with this woman instantly. Pyotor Petrovich does. And yet, there is a certain gravity that dilates this process. Gazing into Lila Rashman's eyes, which he imagines from their amplitudes are green, Pyotor Petrovich feels quite acutely the pain of his wife's loss. One thing has nothing to do with the other, and yet perhaps they are the same—this new beautiful face renewing an old wound of the heart, and especially the memory of another woman, also quite beautiful, who is now long hid among packs of years.

Every night, Pyotor Petrovich sits down to write at the simple pine desk in his apartment. As a young man, he believed that scheduled reflection yielded profoundly therapeutic benefits, and that a mere hour of meditative jotting each day returned to a man many more hours of spiritual equilibrium. Some nights he spends with his journal; on others he composes letters to old friends, or transcribes sections of Pushkin. Tonight, with the light spray of the May rain descending, Pyotor Petrovich writes to Lila Rashman.

He discusses scientific issues, including the most recent American advances in laser optics and how they might profitably be applied to medical technology. The letter doubles as a language lesson. Pyotor Petrovich, whose confidence in his English has been tempered by the American doctor's effortlessly elegant prose, has asked his new correspondent to correct his errors, and to be unflinching in her criticism. He encourages her with a number of purposeful solecisms, "After a hard day of work I am exhaust," and "It is to you that I make question." She finds these, and more. Her grammatical rigor kindles a sort of camaraderie.

And yet, it is not only the grammar. The letters have an indisputable appeal, and they produce a bright excitement that sometimes flowers into joy. Pyotor Petrovich, a man not given to jocosity, finds himself humming a ballad from his student days under his breath. "The river and the afternoon, your arm at rest in mine . . ." He has quite forgotten the rest of the words, although he knows at some point the couple rests in a deep green grove, at which point the boy carves the name of his beloved in the trunk of a young pine. Whenever he had sung the song before, the lovers' circumstance drew Pyotor Petrovich into curious reverie. Were the names still on the tree? Did surface carvings move upward along the trunk as the tree grew in height? Were they covered by the addition of new rings? But this particular morning, as he hums with Lila Rashman in mind, he finds himself suddenly liberated from this line of inquiry, which strikes him as extending well beyond the purview of the tune, and he concentrates instead on the music itself—the periodic rise and fall of the melody, the way that the notes of the chorus cluster in bunches like grapes, the perfect correspondence between the trilling coda and his own lightsome mood. A bumblebee of wadded tape and paper buzzes on the flat top of the file cabinet. He gathers it into his right hand and flings it toward the wastepaper basket, smiling abstractly as it caroms off the rim.

One Monday afternoon, shortly after the weather has thickened in the summer heat, Pyotor Petrovich's older son Vasily comes to visit him at the laboratory. To other men, the two of them must seem quite similar; there is a striking physical resemblance, the same collapsed chin and sharp dark features, the eyes that are the glossy brown of seacoast pebbles. And yet, as men of the world, they could not be more different. As a boy, Vasily had been intelligent but impatient, driven by a burning desire for change that sometimes bordered on despair. As a man, he has become a big wheel in the fledgling world of Soviet advertising, a key figure in the transition from one type of propaganda to the next. Attired like a sharpster in a Botany 500 suit and brushed suede shoes, he is all rude shift, as if a pea has been slipped beneath the mattress of his life. *He* is a rash man. But his energy is contagious, and his rough manner cannot conceal how much he loves his father.

"Ah, so this is your American doctor," Vasily says, tapping the photo, whistling too loudly. "Very easy on the eyes. It's what they call a cocoa tan. I'll bet she has smooth hands and nice curves.

The complexion-and-contour model is all the rage in America these days."

"I have been in communication with her about a very important case for the international research community. You see, a well-respected British scientist accused her team of misconduct." Vasily is uninterested. "Yah, yah."

"The matter is quite serious, I assure you."

"But this picture is more serious to me. Do you deny that she is bewitching? And if you do deny, perhaps you could explain to me why you have put the picture up? Is it covering a hole in the wall?"

"I have a picture of your mother in that same pose."

"What pose? There's no pose in that photography. It's a straight-on head shot." But his son was not looking carefully. Pyotor Petrovich had studied the photograph enough times to recall it to his mind in great detail, and he envisioned her left hand, with its long nails, hovering over the back of the chair, the penumbral rim along the lower edge of her knuckles suggesting a distance of inches between the fingers and the furniture. The picture was taken at a slight angle—the window in the room's rear, which admitted a torrent of white light, was not level with the photographic frame—and the conference table that anchored the scene was unexpectedly foreshortened. A clock on the left wall reads nine.

"I will create an ad campaign for your laboratory. Hop on over to the Drudzgrad-7 Institute. Watch tomorrow's lasers through magic spectacles." He has a great persuasive energy, even though his own conviction is clearly evanescent, and the trained observer in Pyotor Petrovich recognizes the pilgrim under the cynic, the eagerness and even the naïveté in his son's brittle wit. At fifteen, Vasily had travelled to Sofia, and the letters he sent home had convinced Anna that her son was destined to be a great writer. "I am happier than ever," he wrote, "and more uncomfortable than ever. Once your life has taken on the shape of magic, you cannot wait patiently for each individual miracle." Pyotor Petrovich wishes he could warn Vasily of the dangers of his attitude, the folly of embracing extravagant hope, but the thought of his wife softens him. "They are not spectacles," he tells his son, "but special lenses crafted for the testing of new optical technologies."

"You speak like an old woman. The word we print next to it, that is what the world accepts as genuine. Phrase is power." When Pyotor Petrovich announces that he must return to his work, Vasily salutes. "Right, old bean," he says, camouflaging his disappointment with an insincere chipperness. "Do hope to speak with you again some time soon." That night, as he reviews the visit, what surfaces within Pyotor Petrovich is not the barbed comments or the accents, but a single gentle image of Vasily singing, applying a wavery tenor to a popular tune that has drifted over from Prague or Budapest, and before that probably from the West:

> *To kiss a second pair of lips*
> *I know it is a vice*
> *but tell me true what would you do*
> *when she's half as far and twice as nice?*

$\sim$

The next morning, Pyotor Petrovich phones his younger son Jurij, who agrees to visit him in the early afternoon. Once a quiet boy with none of the arrogance of his brother—as a child he had been the very model of modesty and kindness—Jurij has become moody, and sometimes almost inexplicably so, in the last four or five years. Since Anna's death, Pyotor Petrovich knows, the family has endured a vague and general estangement; in a society of men it is inevitable that any individual will feel distant from the fears and hopes of the others, and even from those of his own heart. At times, Vasily has tried to serve the maternal role, calling the three of them together in a rude burlesque of Anna's gossamer diplomacy, and Jurij has resisted those attempts. But this is something different.

Jurij is a concert violinist with one of the finest suburban symphonies, and his music is the most brilliant hue in the spectrum of his young life, a piercing sunflower yellow. At the time of Anna's death, he had just completed his own musical training, and was planning to join the staff of an academy for young prodigies. Anna thought this decision suited him perfectly. "He loves young children so much," she told Pyotor Petrovich, "and is so gentle with them." But after five years at the school, Jurij suddenly submitted his resignation. He was marrying another teacher, a cellist, and the following year, they had a daughter. If Jurij seemed to enjoy his family life at first, there were soon signs of discontent, a bitter gauntness in his manner. Pyotor Petrovich was bothered by this, but he was most troubled by Jurij's growing aversion to Vasily. Whereas he once respected his brother immensely, his attitude now alternated between disdain and envy, and in Vasily's presence he wore a continual sneer that gave him the appearance of a boy on the verge of tears. In the last year or so—since a particularly peevish outburst in which Jurij disparaged Vasily as a "mountebank" and a "rug salesman"—the two had seen each other only rarely, and Pyotor Petrovich did not have the strength to force a reconciliation.

Today, Jurij seems talkative, which Pyotor Petrovich accounts a positive sign until he begins to listen more closely to the content of his son's conversation. It seems he is thinking of leaving Moscow. "I am considering Petersburg," he says, "or perhaps Paris. Somewhere with a well-respected orchestra and some distance from this place. Perhaps that way I can concentrate on my music. These days, when I play, I feel that I am doing nothing but planting myself deeper in mediocrity and sadness." The previous winter, Jurij and his wife had lost a child at twenty weeks, and the miscarriage had strained the marriage greatly. Through Jurij, whose oblique remarks were often quite direct, Pyotor Petrovich gathered that his son suspected Mariana of infidelity, and that he was protecting himself from the consequences by conducting an affair himself.

"Mediocrity?" Pyotor Petrovich says, thinking of Anna, wondering if she monitored the three of them, crisp surveillance pictures delivered to her study in the afterlife. "Nonsense. I've copied out all the praiseworthy bits from last month's Tchaikovsky: 'Impeccable tone,' 'the picture of delicate intensity,' 'the performer's artful domination of the audience.' I even have a picture from the newspaper. There, behind you, to the left of the workbench." Looking at the photograph, Pyotor Petrovich hears the orchestra, the swooping group adagios, the pizzacato of his son's passion singing on the strings. It is hard for him, he admits, to connect that man with the one who stands before him, and harder still to connect either of them with the happy infant who used to gurgle and pinch roundly at his arms. The changes in Jurij these days are like strokes of an oar across the smoky top of a winter lake.

Over the next weeks, his visits become more frequent and more erratic—sometimes a ten-minute chat early in the morning, other times a long and silent appearance that spans the afternoon. One day he stays late, and as he stares at his father with an inscrutable look, Pyotor Petrovich feels as if he were being observed by the ocelli of a peacock. While Vasily is incessant in his commentary—"For the want of a loaf," he might say, tipping *Crime and Punishment* from its station on the bookshelf—Jurij notices nothing, not even the picture of Lila Rashman that counterbalances the picture of him. One day, he asks his father for a camera. This request animates Pyotor Petrovich at once; not only does the mere mention of the device transport him into the past, where he is greeted by dutiful and happy children and a lovely wife, but Jurij's request gives him the opportunity to hold forth on his newest invention. With a happy laugh, he produces a small black box, no larger than a cigarette pack, with a panel of buttons stretching across its top. This is the plain-paper camera, a device that transfers black-and-white photographs to ordinary white paper in the manner of a xerographic copier. He has had great success with it lately—though the images produced are of inferior quality, the process compensates with its incredibly low cost—and has begun to dream of marketing it, rueing his dreams of wealth even as he dreams them, knowing how foolish they must be. "I hope that it brings you pleasure," says Pyotor Petrovich, proffering the camera with a flourish. His son returns a grim indecipherable smile.

With his only promising invention loaned out, Pyotor Petrovich wraps himself tighter in his epistolary flirtation, feeling as he did when he was a young man. He pulls a footstool into the closet and retrieves from a high shelf a box of stationery, a gift to him from his wife in the year of her death. The beautiful golden hue of the paper has since faded, but it has left behind a pattern, a comfortable honeyed grain. It is proper, and even generous, to write his letters on this paper. It will remind him of his strongest moments, and help him validate them.

Lila. He writes it and then stops. He paces his apartment, singing, the freshness of the music almost indecent, like the sharp sweet swell of a newly mown meadow. In Britain he once developed a passion for a radio singer named Lily Atamasco, but this is an unfamiliar variation. Lila. He pronounces it sometimes in bed as a private enjoyment, feeling quite silly, but attempting the American accents, elongating the *i* until it is a long staircase of gentle grade and the *l*'s newels at either end, with the *a* an exhaled afterthought, a foot-carpet thrown by the bottommost riser. Spoken in the dark of his bedroom, a close and treacly dark more green than black, her name is a stream, cool and subtle, purling in his throat. Lila. Under the spell of these two syllables, each the imperfect copy of the other, together a perfect pair, his work begins to change. He is less methodical and less patient, finds himself daydreaming in ways he has not in forty years—hung up on a vague memory of the first line of "Novogodnee," an unfamiliar raven-haired figure glimpsed from behind—and then finds the daydreams alternating with flashes of brilliant intuition. What would Rostikov think? Would he scorn this intuitive turn as sophistry and sorcery? When Pyotor Petrovich attempts the mental transport that usually brings him closer to the man, his memory is of a portly figure rather pontifical than authoritative, and with an affected orotundity that verges on the comical. One night he dreams that he portrays his old mentor in a skit, and that he waxes the ends of his costume-moustache until his eyes are wet with laughing tears. He knows he is performing for someone, that he is showing off, and when he wakes in the morning he can do nothing but lie grinning in his bed. The dreamer and the scientist are warring within him, and victory is falling to the dreamer.

It is early on a Tuesday morning when Jurij calls the flat. "Father," he says, and nothing else. Pyotor has not even had his toast and coffee.

"Jurij," he says. No response. He repeats his son's name, searches for him in the interminable silence. Still nothing. His heart thudding, Pyotor Petrovich sighs to calm himself and delivers a sugared homily. "Jurij, listen to me. Whatever is troubling you, it will pass. You are very young still, and look upon such difficulties as permanent. I have more experience with these things. Please, Jurij, I cannot talk to you now. The bus for work is leaving shortly. But come by and see me this afternoon."

Finally, Jurij answers. "I will." But Pyotor waits into the evening, staring at the wall clock and the newspaper photo of Jurij beneath it, and finally leaves shortly after seven. The next day Ivan Zaitsev, the lab director, informs him that the equipment office cannot account for a small amount of money. It has been accounted lost, but there are suspicions of theft, directed chiefly at Old Ganev, who has guided his mop listlessly around the corners of the lab for almost twenty years now. It is only later, when he returns to his small apartment, that he remembers Jurij's phone call, and feels a sick tug at his stomach as he wonders if perhaps his younger son subscribes to a very different standard of conduct from that which he has upheld all his life.

∾

Two weeks later—weeks that have passed without any sign of Jurij, who continues to schedule visits he does not keep—a small fire breaks out in a laboratory down the hall, and spreads through I-9. Arriving in the morning, Pyotor Petrovich finds one of the Kopfverdrehers clucking in the security area. "What's the matter?" he asks, and is answered only by stern Teutonic silence. In his lab, a sooty patina has settled over the floor and workbench. His bookshelf attests to a critical precision in the flames' encroachment; the Dostoevsky is damaged, but the Puskhin barely touched. It is not until nine that he notices his greatest loss—the two newsprint photographs that flanked his workbench are gone, and where they hung there are now only nails ringed by collars of carbonized paper. He finds a single scrap that must have been blown free of the flames and handles it as reverently as the palmer treats his leaves. She is not in it, only the face of a man who stood to her rear right, but he knows her in the man's aspect. That night, he writes with greater urgency, heedless of his grammar and dependent on his intensity to navigate him safely through. He reports the fire, even ventures an explanation that he will admit to no one else—"I am afraid that my son is somehow involved in the cause"—and concludes with a request divested of his usual playful manner. "My dear Doctor Rashman, I would like from you a replacement of the photograph. Or else I should feel as if there is nothing firm beneath my feet."

Another round of visits by his sons. Again, Vasily comes first, volume turned high, pressuring his father to help him invest in a new business. "Oh, that's right, father. You don't know what business is. How could you? When have you seen true industry at work? The hot blood of capital flowing freely."

He hardly has the energy to spar, but he makes a valiant attempt, fearful that if he does not, Vasily will sense his preoccupation, and ferret out its source. "I was once a visitor in Berlin."

"Ach, Berlin. Jelly doughnuts. I am speaking of America. Bruce Springsteen. Michael Jackson. Julia Roberts. Abundancies you cannot dream of. Once more, into the broil. Your ideas will make us men thick with money." From his tone, it is apparent that it is more than mere cupidity that powers this vision of a life transformed. It is pride in his father, and it is love.

Shortly after Vasily departs, singing another American

song, Jurij arrives. He enters without ceremony, Pyotor Petrovich's camera extended before him, and despite the shaky smile on his face, his struggle with his demons has apparently been to lamentable purpose, for he looks dissipated and afraid, with a terrible unevenness to his gaze. Shortly after he arrives he bends over the wastebasket and spits noisily into its depths, an insanity. "Father," he says, and then pauses, steadying himself against the workbench. His smile is gone now and his starched shirt collar pretends to cut his throat. "I have two favors to ask."

"Yes."

"What I need," he resumes, "is for you to hold something for me." He produces a thin manila envelope. "This contains some extremely important documents that need safekeeping until next month." Pyotor Petrovich accepts the envelope without comment and, as his son watches, places it in a file drawer. "Good," says Jurij. "Also, I need more money. Do you have some I could borrow?" Pyotor Petrovich silently gestures toward the top drawer of the desk. Jurij slides out a few bills, and conveys them to a front pocket of his pants. There is something in the gesture that strikes Pyotor Petrovich as professional. He does not ask his son questions, but lets him speak, and speak he does, about his wife, how he loves her, how he hopes that his life regains its balance. "And little Julia," he says, "she is growing so quickly that I close my eyes sometimes to keep an image of her. Yesterday I lay on the ground and held her up flying until my arms hurt." The memory brushes his features with a faint happiness, and Pyotor Petrovich remembers how his son had looked at birth, at two, on the first day of school, on his wedding night. Openmouthed, seemingly on the verge of explaining what it is that troubles him, Jurij suddenly colors a deep red, and then that color, too, drains from his face, and he leaves the lab without speaking.

That night Pyotor Petrovich writes a long letter to Lila Rashman, a confession of sorts that telescopes his paternity into a few representative incidents—Vasily's birth, a minor ice-skating accident when Jurij was eight, the stark mystery of that afternoon's visit. "I do not know what to do. He will not confide in me, and his fear frightens me terribly. All children must grow, and so, too, have my sons, although as men they are leaving me emptier than ever." He intends this lament as a declaration of love, and after rereading the letter copies it into his journal, so nakedly does it present his feelings. He does not, however, mail it.

The following week he spends his evenings in the laboratory, each night staying later than the one before. He eats less and less, not out of diet any longer but because he is not hungry, and one night he realizes with that he is pining over the letter he has not mailed, pining like a schoolboy, and that he will not regain his equilibrium until he knows, in some small way, that Lila Rashman understands the extent of his feelings for her. Thursday night he is tinkering with the camera when he hears a faint noise somewhere in the building, a distant plashing of glass. Ganev, he thinks to himself. Senile. Should tell Ivan Zaitsev. Pyotor Petrovich returns to the camera, and he is probing in its empty stomach with a tweezer, trying to separate two capacitors, when a terrible scraping fills the room. His glance flies to the peephole. Someone is at the laboratory door. He reaches for the telephone, but the lights are suddenly dimmed, and a streak of grey enters his field of vision. Wild, panicked, he gropes for his glasses, spilling a flask of water onto Jurij's envelope, overturning a lamp, and then incongruously, even delicately, depressing the small red button atop the camera. Click. The image is of an older man, his eyes bright with terror, a scream sliding from between his thin concluding lips. A moment later darkness descends with the speed of a shutter.

~

Vasily will never forget that night. He had a girl at his apartment, a delicious blonde from the firm, and with the help of two bottles of Romanian wine, he had divested her of her blouse and begun to explore the thrilling heat seeping from beneath her skirt.

Fortune, he remembers thinking, is kissing me once more. And then the phone rang. "I am sorry to bother you at home," said the voice, "but there has been an incident in the Drudzgrad-7 lab."

"My father," said Vasily. "Is he hurt?"

"No," said the detective, and Vasily felt relief mingled with annoyance—if not hurt, then why the disturbance—a relief that was quickly obliterated by the force of the clarification. "He is dead."

At the lab, Vasily wept openly in the room that no longer contained his father's body, the spilled water, the overturned lamp. Why would anyone kill this man? Had his behavior been strange? the detective asked. Not at all, Vasily reponded. But he knew that this was not quite true. His father's behavior had been strange. He had been in love.

In the year since he founded the Stuttgart-based Patersen Camerawerkes, Vasily himself has ripened; he has become an important man with a serious manner, a large office, a larger home, and an imperiously beautiful German fiancée. Many days, he cannot believe the change that time has wrought, and he sneaks away with a secretary. Other days, he patrols the office proudly, especially the lobby area, anchored by a photograph of Pyotor Petrovich retrieved from the X-3 prototype the morning after his death. This photograph—grainier than the prints the cameras now produce, but a respectable predecessor nonetheless—has an appropriately memorial flavor, although no one, not even Vasily, imagines the grisly circumstances of its production.

The company is a great success, one of the largest suppliers of personal cameras in Eastern Europe, and its rise is followed with interest by the international press. Hungry for stories of post-Communist accomplishment amid the myriad examples of fracture and failure, journalists are drawn to Patersen Camera not only by its balance sheet but also by the young and charismatic president whose financial success conceals two personal tragedies—the murder of his father and the mysterious death of his brilliant younger brother. Selections from Pyotor Petrovich's journals, made public under Vasily's supervision, often accompany articles; the corporation owes its humanistic philosophy,

Vasily insists repeatedly in print, to his father. As the first anniversary of the Stuttgart plant approaches, Vasily asks a young German reporter who has recently written on the company if his paper would be interested in the correspondence between Pyotor Petrovich and an American research scientist. "It's a touching story," he says. "He felt so deeply for her, and they never met. We give all of our employees a week's paid vacation when they are married. Her name was Lila Rashman. I will try to contact her if you like, and give your paper an exclusive."

He felt so deeply for her. How deeply? And did she feel for him? Vasily muses on these questions, framing possible answers, on-the-record answers, as the overseas operator patches him transatlantic, as the American operator retrieves the call, as the secretary in the chemistry department places him on hold, and then she is on the line, a pleasant voice with flattened vowels and a quizzical cast. "This is Lila Rashman." He introduces himself. "My father was a scientist in Moscow. He corresponded with you a few years ago. I wonder if you might remember him."

"Of course I remember your father. We had written to one another a few times, and then his letters stopped. Has something happened? Has he lost his job?"

"He has lost more than his job." It is a stupid thing to say, characteristic of his love of cleverness over kindness, and it verges on a cruelty toward this stranger who cares for his dead father. She lets out a soft cry. "You don't mean he's . . ."

"Yes, I'm afraid so." He has regained control now, his consonants rolling, continental and persuasive, his speech the speech of the man he always knew he would become. "A rather tragic case, something in his laboratory. My father was killed by an intruder. It was very difficult for us at first, but easier now. He spoke often of you."

"Yes," she says. There is still a wariness in her voice. "How strange that you should call me now. I will be in Prague this April for a conference, and I was considering phoning your father."

"Prague," he repeats. "How wonderful. You must come to Stuttgart. You will be my guest."

She arrives just before lunch, accompanied by another American doctor. After a round of introductions, the man excuses himself, reminding her that he be at the station at seven. She sits in Vasily's office, brushing her skirt nervously, and the two of them begin to talk. She is forty-two, ten years divorced, childless, an avid crossword hobbyist. She loves her work. Her traveling companion is a man who believes she will agree to marry him. She will not. Vasily nods ruefully. I understand completely, he says. I have an engagement myself that I may be breaking shortly. I have found myself sometimes satisfied with only the shallow portions of myself. My father was murdered and my brother, too, is dead. They eat in the company cafeteria, Vasily making a show of his good rapport with even the lowest employees. "Hello, Karl," he says to the burly cashier. "Is your son's twisted ankle healed? He is a smart boy who should not be playing with the roughnecks." Lila Rashman laughs. Late in the afternoon, after an hour of wine has created a provisional intimacy—an intimacy assisted, they both know, by the fact that they will never again see one another—Vasily asks her if she knew his father loved her. She lifts her eyes to his without answering, and a mix of pain and passion flickers in their middle depths. "Would you like to see a photograph of him?" asks Vasily, and she nods.

He takes her to the lobby; a company photographer is waiting. Lila Rashman stands silent before the showcase, shifting. The main lamp has switched to evening wattage, suffusing the case's contents with a yellow melancholy. "I thought he would look different," she says. As she stares at the photo, Vasily permits himself to stare at her. Even teeth. Long black hair. Complexion and contour. He marvels at his father's boldness; she really is quite beautiful. The photographer arranges the pair before the case and snaps once, twice, a third time, each click accompanied by the pop of a recyclable flashbulb manufactured in the Stuttgart facility. Two of the photos are published the next morning alongside an article about the company's first birthday; Lila Rashman is mentioned in a caption as "a friend and colleague of the late Pyotor Petrovich." There will come a time when nothing is left of the picture but an ashen ghost haunting scraps of newsprint. But for now, forever, the two of them together gaze up as at an altar, into the magnified image, grand in modesty and kindness, of Pyotor Petrovich's dead face.

IV. Oh, Mama! Chapter One

In which I set out to write a novel detailing my unsteady course through life, which began promisingly in the cosseted suburbs of Baltimore, Maryland; moved through a childhood characterized by the sturdy but not overbearing love of both parents and the evident but not embarrassing admiration of a younger sister; rocketed through an entertaining and rewarding adolescence filled with academic, cultural, and athletic achievement that was shattered irretrievably by the death in a car accident of my younger sister when she was sixteen and I was eighteen; spent six months mourning her, not only in death, but mourning her retroactively in life, as it became apparent after her accident that she was hardly the model of sweetness and decorum I thought I knew but instead a rather wild girl who was, at the time of her accident, sky-high on angel dust and going down on a thirty-two-year-old real-estate agent who was in the process of driving her to a model house in Virginia for their regularly scheduled Thursday afternoon tryst; paused briefly in a hospital, not physical but mental, for exhaustion brought on by recurring dreams of murdering the real-estate agent, who was cleared of all charges in the accident and went on to become something of a tycoon in the neighborhood, developing several townhouse complexes, including the one in which I now live; then picked up again with a series of entertainingly self-destructive romances, one succeeding the other in such rapid succession that, viewed together they acquire the feel of silent screen comedy; and finally came to rest on the smooth, cool brow of a woman I met in a flower shop. (I was there buying flowers for another woman, a woman who was in fact my wife, but whose goodwill toward me had grown so attenuated that calling her my wife was akin to calling a dog who was biting me "my pet." (I told her this once and she said, "Are you comparing me to a fucking dog?" and then she threw a cigarette lighter at me, lit, though it lost its flame the second it left her hand.)) I took the flower shop woman to dinner the following week (we found that we made each other laugh, and that we looked somewhat good together in the mirror behind the bar); took her to bed the week after that (I must say that my performance was poor, due primarily to the fact that for weeks I had been making a habit, each night, of drinking a half-dozen rum and cokes, which my doctor was later to tell me was laughably destructive to what he euphemistically called my "physical well-being," given that it robbed me of proper sleep and also introduced a mild toxin into my bloodstream); saw her decreasingly for a few months and then, for six months, not at all (she told a mutual acquaintance that she was not sure what she felt, but that she was sure that she felt enough negative things to outweigh any positive ones, and the mutual acquaintance, being a sadist, related the news to me promptly); then ran into her in a movie theater; then began to see again, first for a few friendly meals, then romantically once again (this time with markedly better results); and then, hoping against hope, my heart clutched like a fist, in a small upstate inn at which I proposed an arrangement, not marriage exactly, given that I was still somewhat married, but an understanding in which she and I would spend a single evening together each week, building on our goodwill, ignoring the fact that I was still in something of a muddle and that she not only had the same name as my sister, but shared her hair color, her bell-when-struck laugh, and her penchant for lovely, if expensive, shirts that accentuated the shape of her body, particularly her breasts (the woman, not my sister, though I suppose it was true in my sister's case as well, despite the fact that I tried my hardest not to think of my sister as a sexual being, even after the facts of her death came to light (let me also mention that this woman knew that she had wonderful breasts, or, as she liked to say, "grade-A tits," and that she wasn't too shabby in the other departments either)), all contributing to a similarity between the two women that, had I had any foresight at all, I would have seen as psychologically problematic (and that's not even counting the fact that this woman was, by any objective standard, a hard case, given to fits of rage and petulance, somewhat entitled, high in dudgeon but also, underneath the armor, sweet and perceptive and affectionate, if also somewhat self-conscious about her sexuality (when she was single, she once told me, she used to arrange evenings in which she masturbated in each room in the house, to which I said, drolly, "Even the bedroom?")), but instead ignored and moved blindly forward on a . . . cloud? . . .no . . . a raft? . . . no . . .a flying carpet of goodwill, trusting that my love for her would at length prevail.

V. The Theft of a Knife

Editor's Note:

The earliest of the chapters in this novel—a draft of which existed as far back as his graduate years—"The Theft of a Knife" illustrates Mr. Greenman's obsession with the American West. As a student, he began at least two novels set on the far side of the Continental Divide: a novel about rebirth set in Phoenix, Arizona, and a novel about terminal illness set in Dyer, Nevada. Neither was completed—the region, while adequately symbolic, was evidently not adequately inspirational. Then he wrote this, which he mentioned to me in a note: "Finally, I have bested the West." This piece marks the first occurrence of what would become a common trope in Mr. Greenman's work: the creation of a false editor who shadows the author figure. Here the author is in dispute, and the editor is seeking to resolve that dispute: more specifically, past annotators and academics have created doubt as to whether the author is the Australian memoirist Christina Handel or the American poet Don Herman (both of whom are inventions of Mr. Greenman's), and the editor seems certain that he knows the answer.

In devising this two-tiered structure in which an editor mediates the reader's experience of a text, did Mr. Greenman foresee that he would one day require my help, the way that early psychoanalysis held that the ego anticipates the super-ego? It seems likely that psychoanalysis is at the heart of this piece, for two reasons. First, there is the fact that the seed of this story lay in an episode in which a romantic acquaintance of Mr. Greenman's stole from him a biography of Freud. Apparently, the two of them had been shopping for housewares for the young lady's apartment, which Mr. Greenman visited frequently, and he set his book down on a table and asked her to watch after it while he fetched a clerk. When he returned, the book was gone, and she was apologetic; weeks later he found it under her bed, hidden in a paper bag. Secondly, there is the fact of Mr. Greenman's thoroughgoing preoccupation with knives, which finds its earliest articulation in this story. When I was teaching Mr. Greenman, I remember lecturing the class on an episode in Jung's youth in which a séance ended when a bread knife exploded into four pieces. It is not possible that Mr. Greenman does not remember this story, as he came to me after the class and expressed a fascination with it. And while it is possible that many readers will respond to the symbol of the knife—its phallic connotations are well known—I cannot help but feel that it is intended specifically for me. A reference such as this is like a chain that binds two people. Much time can be spent just feeling the links.

∿

Bartlett Adamson has made the point that Christina Handel's posthumously published novel Not Now; I'm Not Hungry *is actually three novels. The first two sections of* Not Now; I'm Not Hungry *offer semiautobiographical accounts of the author's own life, the first from the perspective of a spirited Canberra girl of fourteen coping with her parents' divorce, and the second from the vantage of a woman of thirty-five thrown into crisis by the unexpected reappearance of an ex-lover. The third, and shortest, part of the novel differs from these first two drastically. Titled "The Knife Takes Its First Steps toward Manhood," it sounds many of the same notes as Jorge Luis Borges's classic short story "The South," telling the tale of a young American man who moves out West with the hopes of beginning a new life. Attenuated in its syntax where Handel is usually telegraphic, sparse in its imagery where Handel is usually lush, remote from the rest of Handel's oeuvre in both its themes and its settings, this section of the novel has given critics pause since the work's publication, and most have assumed that it represented a new direction for Handel that she would have pursued had she not overdosed on a combination of barbiturates and alcohol in July 1993. Adamson, writing in the* New Australian Review *in*

September of that same year, is as usual an accurate barometer of the prevailing opinion: "So different is 'The Knife Takes Its First Steps toward Manhood' from the balance of Not Now; I'm Not Hungry, so opposite in its method, subject, and sensibility, we can surmise only that Handel was beginning a brave inquiry into the circularity of existence, that she was activating the political commonplace that a rightmost extreme is so rightmost that it becomes leftmost, and activating it to ascend into new paradoxes—freedom as confinement, barbarism as civilization, youth as age, placement as displacement, and honesty as deceit."

Like all critical claims about the authorial intentions of dead writers, this assumption is thoroughly unanswerable. New evidence, however, suggests that it is also thoroughly unconvincing. Last month, a London rare book dealer with an interest in Australian literature, and particularly contemporary Australian women's literature, purchased from the collector Thomas Gettelman a mothballed collection of leather-bound volumes once owned by Handel. While dusting the cover of Francis Bacon's New Atlantis *(a book Gettelman never troubled to open), the dealer found pressed between pages a letter sent to Handel in September 1989 from an American poet named Don Herman, with whom she was romantically involved during her time in Atlanta in 1985 and 1986. In the three-page, handwritten letter, Herman asks after Handel's health, particularly her mental health—the series of nervous breakdowns that would eventually trigger her suicide had begun in the summer of 1988— and encourages her to visit him in Boston. "We can sit up late and naked and play the summer cannibal game, laying in the cut of the sheets. We can watch the harbor through my window, which has broad, brown curtains that swell grandly in the breeze. Does it appeal?"*

Toward the end of the letter, Herman turns away from the personal toward the professional, noting excitedly that "I have finished another series of poems, this time mostly about silverware—as mirrors, as utensils, as anthropomorphs (who among us has not imagined himself a spoon, knife, or fork?)" "Hey, Tina," he writes in conclusion, addressing Handel by her pet name, "I have been striking some prose poses also, and have finished my story of cowboy Bruce, and how from utter hope he passes into a state of almost abject hopelessness, all as a result of a hasty judgment and an empty bag. I have enclosed this story, for your enjoyment, and as always cannot wait to hear whether it satiates or leaves you famished." In The Collected Correspondence of Christina Handel (University of California Press, 1995), there is no record of this letter, or any response to it, and while there are dozens of earlier letters sent from Handel to Herman and Herman to Handel, no later correspondence exists (indeed, within months it would have become impossible, since Herman died in a boating accident in January 1990). Encouraged by this recent find, librarians at the Sydney University holdings department located among another set of Handel papers a typewritten manuscript previously considered a draft of the final episode of Not Now; I'm Not Hungry. The marginal handwriting on the manuscript, matching in part that of Herman's letters, suggests that this is most likely the "story of cowboy Bruce," despite the fact that the main character is named Lukke.

The question of whether Don Herman is in fact the original author of this piece, and, if so, how Herman's fiction came to be part of Handel's novel, is a perplexing one. Did Handel incorporate Herman's fiction into her own effort without his permission? Did she publish it for him as a sort of memorial tribute? Or is it possible that an overzealous publisher's assistant found the episode among Handel's papers at her death and absorbed it into the massive work-in-progress without carefully examining its provenance? Whatever the case, it seems fair to re-present "The Knife Takes Its First Steps toward Manhood" here, with this additional bit of context restored. One final curiosity: Scholars of Handel, and in fact any careful reader familiar with Not Now; I'm Not Hungry will note that the final paragraph of this version of the piece differs from the version that appears in the novel. The differences are not conspicuous—they consist of two simple typographical variants in the last sentence—but they are significant,

transposing concrete nouns and abstract ones and echoing the
philosophical notes sounded earlier in the piece. Whether the dif-
ference between the two versions is the result of conscious alter-
ations by Handel or another typesetter's intervention, we may
never know. The fiction, however, persists on its own merits.

∼

The young man who set out for the Six Hills Ranch in West
Rock, Wyoming, in 1891 bore the name of Lukke Major, and while
he was trained as an appraiser of beautiful things—of French
engravings, in specific—he considered himself more of a rugged
adventurer. His parents were prominent members of St. Louis's
Baptist community, and left their two sons with a substantial
inheritance at their death in 1890, requesting that they stay in
Missouri and become doctors or clergymen. The elder brother,
Marshall Major, followed the spirit of the request if not the letter,
eventually gaining renown as a restaurateur across the Midwest.
But Lukke Major was not particularly mindful of his heritage.
Intoxicated by extravagant dreams of his own freedom, he used
half of his leavings to purchase a small farm on the Wyoming
plain, and spent the winter transporting himself mentally across
the intervening miles. He saw the brown of the farmhouse, the
gold of the surrounding fields, the cerulean blue of the Western
sky, and saw in the sky what looked like angels in benevolent rota-
tion, protecting his new farm, his grand and hopeful plan.

In St. Louis, while his brother Marshall worked as a cook and
his sister Grace married an older lawyer whose garlicky mustache
gainsaid an otherwise winning personality, Lukke lived a life of
indolence and dissipation, drifting from woman to woman and
tavern to tavern, reading Poe and the penny sheets, telling all
who would listen that the West was a lace of boundless opportunity for a man as keen and brave as he. And then, late in 1891,
he set off for West Rock to claim what he had bought. He took
with him very little—apart from the financial paperwork and the
letter of guarantee which attested to his ownership of the ranch,

both of which he kept neatly folded and filed in a leather grip-sack, he carried only a few shirts, a spare pair of shoes, a philos-ophy primer, a black Stetson he had purchased in a haberdashery for nine dollars, and seven thousand dollars in cash. He liked to say that he valued the primer and the hat both above the cash, although this was not even close to true.

The trip from St. Louis to Wyoming began on a Monday morning. He had spent the night before in the company of cheap red wine and a young woman who was considerably more costly. Her name was Marianna, and she claimed that she was from a good family that had fallen on bad times. "Just like the human race," Lukke had asked, laughing the bitter laugh of a man who thinks he has been granted wisdom in his youth. Lukke had been with ladies of the night before, but for some reason he was feel-ing especially intimate with this one, and he imagined that she was his young wife, filled with desire and hate for him, both at once. When he asked her to wear his hat, she started and cried that she would not want to be a man, although she wouldn't say why. In the morning, Lukke took his suitcase and his gripsack (his money stacked nearly underneath his contracts and his letter of guarantee), and left.

The train station was an assembly of solitaries, the early hour demanding a personality remote from companions, a bit touched, or—in Lukke's case—enamored of adventure. The train itself was new, and Lukke felt he was being treated to a glimpse of the future. Everything shone. Not fifteen minutes outside of St. Louis, the sight of a bird pecking at the stomach of a dead dog threw a scare into him. He wondered if it was an omen, and his optimism dimmed sharply. He consoled himself by reading Hume, and reminding himself that there was no causality but simply adjacent relations. If I push this book from my lap, he thought to himself the book falls to the ground. But I cannot say with certainty that my push causes the fall. If I scream loudly, others may come running to my aid. But I cannot say with cer-tainty that my scream caused them to assist me. If I wait here long enough, others will enter my compartment. But I cannot say with certainty that my waiting caused the others to arrive. He entertained a seemingly endless series of false causes and effects, and at length sleep came, although he could not say with certainty that his exhaustion contributed materially.

The men who woke him came into the compartment separately, perhaps ten minutes apart, the first predictably sitting himself in the bench opposite Lukke, the second standing in the doorway and surveying the two half-occupied benches before deciding to cast his lot with the recent arrival—though he could not have known he was a recent arrival—rather than Lukke. The second man was small and burly, the first tall and lanky; both wore bowlers, and had watch fobs dangling from their vest pockets. Lukke hung on the edge of his sleep, watched the two men enter, watched them sit, watched the tall man write a letter and smoke a meerschaum pipe, and the small man file his fingernails and test his breath against a cupped palm. After the stop in Topeka it was afternoon, shadows lengthening against the flat bright plains, and all three men relaxed enough to speak to one another. The small man introduced himself first, as Edward Brockner, an investigator for a rival railway company. He was entrusted with the safety of certain types of postal deliveries. It was all he would say about his work; "Later," he promised, "I will say more." The large man was Edward St. John, a solicitor from Boston on his way to San Francisco to oversee the establishment of a new branch of a lending institution. They spoke for a bit, Lukke explaining that he was going to the West to manage a newly acquired property and to find a wife—he had not thought about the matter of marriage before, but as he spoke it occurred to him that it was probably true. "Later," he said, "I, too, will say more." Brockner laughed, and St. John laughed too.

In the morning the fraternity of the car was upset somewhat when a woman entered and rode from Denver; she was a woman of strange appearance, unhealthily thin, with a shock of jet-black hair and a back that curved as it rose, reminding Lukke of St. Louis's wrought-iron lampposts. But her face was quite pretty, and her manner pleasant, and since Lukke felt himself to be a man of the world, a man who could speak easily to a woman of any background, he struck up a conversation with the new arrival. Brockner and St. John tucked their chins into their chests and slept. Brockner snored. The woman gave her name as Paula Ray, and said that she was a lady of the theater. "Not an actress, I'm afraid," she said. "Rather, I write."

"That's wonderful," said Lukke. "I am not often in the theater."

"All the new plays are about theft," she said. "In this they resemble the old plays."

Somewhere in the mountains the train stopped, and Lukke stepped out with Paula Ray, careful to take his hat and his gripsack with him. The two of them promenaded around the little town, which had a hot springs and a general store. In the store, Lukke bought himself a pipe. He didn't smoke, but he assumed he would soon begin to do so. Gallantly, he offered to make a present of a hat to Miss Ray. She accepted, and picked out a woolen cap that fit snugly atop her head. It was the same black color as her hair, and the same color as the bench near the train station where they went to sit at the conclusion of their walk. At their feet, the afternoon shadows dropped out as dusk encroached.

Feeling bold, Lukke asked Paula Ray if she had a man somewhere. "A beau," he said, when she looked confused. "Or are there many suitors?"

She stared down into the dusk. "No," she said finally. "I was married once. My husband died. I don't imagine that I will ever marry again."

Lukke started to speak, but found he had nothing to say. There had been a kind of certainty in her voice that outflanked him. He just stared at the joint where her hat met her hair until the conductor called for them to board. She did not return to sit in Lukke's compartment.

Just after Salt Lake City, Brockner broke out a deck of cards and some whiskey in celebration. They played poker, and while the other men held their cards casually, Lukke kept his close to his neck, almost touching his Adam's apple. "If the lady had stayed, we could have enjoyed a round of whist," St. John said, sniggering, and Brockner coughed into his own hand once again. Lukke was not much of a card player, but the stakes were low, pocket money only, and he quite enjoyed the camaraderie he felt with his two traveling mates, not to mention the cordial burn of Brockner's whiskey. After St. John won his third straight hand, with a queens-high full house, Brockner bore upon the others to listen to a story. "I said I would say more about my line of work," he said, "and now I mean to make good on that promise." While he was in Cincinnati, he said, he had known a man who worked for more than thirty years as a master engineer. Thirty years of distinguished service, commendations, the respect of his superiors and the adulation of those to whom he was superior. And then, one spring, he stole a knife from the foot locker of another man who was threatening to use it against a young switchman who had sassed him. The master engineer was dismissed. "He was a close acquaintance, if not exactly a friend of mine," said Brockner, "and yet I could not defend him. He had a system at his disposal, a way to report a wrongful act being plotted. Instead, he took matters into his own hands, and it was it own hands that did him in."

"Aristotle would say that the knife caused the man to steal it," Lukke said.

"What?" Brockner said. "Who's that, son?"

"Aristotle. The Greek philosopher. He thought that the plants caused the rain to fall as a way of getting nourishment."

St. John gave a rude laugh. "You should move on to more modern thinking. It's clear that the newspapers cause the rain to fall as a way of using up the space they have reserved for writing about the weather."

"I never read the newspaper," said Brockner. "In fact, I never read much of anything anymore. I once was a voracious reader, but I gave it all up after a while."

"You stopped reading?" Lukke said.

"Yes, I did," Brockner said. "At some point, it seemed to me that there was no yield in it. It wasn't that I felt that the things I was reading weren't saying anything. It's that I felt they were saying everything. One book might say that a man died when he fell from a horse. Another might say that he was crushed by his disappointment and died of a broken heart. If I do not know this man, how do I know which is true? A string of words on a piece of paper is nothing more than a lie that most men believe."

"In the law," St. John said, "it is a lie that all men believe."

Lukke ran a hand along his own leg. He was numb and more than a little drunk. He had been mumbling to himself mostly, the whisky a somnolent trickle in his belly, and hadn't intended to speak so loudly. He sat in silence for a few minutes, and then lurched to his feet and retrieved the gripsack from the compartment overhead. "I have something to show you two fellows," he said. "You are fine fellows, and friends of mine now, so I want to show you where I am going and how I plan to make my life." He fumbled in the gripsack for the letter from the bank in West Rock. "I have a small farm that I own in Wyoming. They are expecting me. I have a guarantee." He held up the letter, which wavered in his hand. Brockner and St. John smiled at him. Returning the letter to the gripsack, he felt around for his money, which he also wanted to show the men. It was gone. "What's the idea?" he said, taking up his hat nervously. "I had some money in here. Where has it gone?"

"How much money?" said St. John.

"Quite a bit," said Lukke. "It was an inheritance."

"Have you seen it since Salt Lake City?" Brockner asked. Lukke thought of the strange woman who had shared their compartment. A pain went through his stomach, and doubled him over.

"Let's get you to the rail detective's office," said Brockner, and Lukke took his hand. St. John steadied Lukke along his right side. His hat was in his other hand like a periapt. The two men helped him out of the car and turned toward the back of the train. Halfway down the hallway, he began to ask again about the money, louder this time. Maybe his friends would help him, go searching for the woman from car to car. Surely Brockner knew how to conduct an investigation. "Don't fall," said Brockner. "The detectives are always in the last car." St. John had him by the coat, and Lukke couldn't have fallen if he had wanted to, so tight was the man's grip on his sleeve. He held his own hat just as tightly.

Saying nothing, the men pushed Lukke into the last car, which was not an office but a baggage car. St. John kicked open a door, and the train was suddenly filled with the whoosh of the ground rushing by. Brockner pulled out his watch fob. At the end of the chain there was no watch, only a flat metal rectangle that Lukke soon saw was a folding knife. With one motion, Brockner pierced Lukke's thin coat and shirt, buried the blade in the shallows of his belly, and pulled upward. With a sharp gasp, Lukke pulled the knife out and slashed at Brockner, but St. John was already upon him, choking him. Lukke dropped his hat to the floor of the car, and then was knocked down beside it by a thunderous blow from St. John. He felt at his stomach with his free hand, which came away sticky with blood, and then took his hat in his hand again. Brockner, whose face was twisted into an angry smile, threw Lukke's gripsack off—it exploded when it hit the ground, sending papers everywhere—and St. John threw Lukke off. He landed in a bed of briars, whimpering from the pain, but did not stop, simply rolled over and crawled toward the gripsack, which was wedged into underbrush near the top of a small knoll. Halfway there, a rustling noise drew his gaze downward, and there he saw his contracts for the ranch in West Rock, his dreams rendered in vellum, his future printed formally on a half-dozen envelopes. Lukke lifted one page and tried to read it, but the wind folded a corner and he could not. Re-placing it on the ground, he covered it, and the others, stubbornly. They would not move now, the papers. They would never say anything other than what they said now. The ranch was his. The pain in his stomach was dull, and as small as the receding train, as he looked around him, at the knoll,and a small creek over the hill, and a redbird in a high tree branch. Not dead but maybe dying, and wondering whether he could say with any certainty that dying was a cause of death, Lukke lay there, a knife in one hand, his hat in his other, face down in the guarantee.

VI. In the Presence of the General

In the presence of the General, I scratch my nose. It doesn't itch, so I'm not sure why I'm doing this. Maybe I'm nervous.

The General calls the Colonel, who has a coil of rope. "Here," the General says, throwing me one end. I pull. The General pulls. We've been through this before.

Later, much later, after the pulling stops, the Colonel and I go to visit my wife, who lives in an apartment with my baby. I don't live there anymore. But we're on good terms, me and the wife and the baby. My wife is busy with a knife and some celery, but she sets her work aside and offers glasses of iced tea to me and the Colonel. He accepts, but he won't drink it. I know he won't. That guy never drinks anything, best as I can tell, or eats anything either. It's amazing that he keeps his strength. But in that rope-pulling competition he never loses, except when he pulls against the General. You don't show up the General. The reason is rank. The reason is obvious.

My wife pours our tea, hers and mine and the Colonel's, into three identical glasses. The baby has its own glass, which is smaller and has flowers all over it and has a rubber stopper-top and is actually plastic. My wife fills that with apple juice. The baby slaps the table with open hands to show how much it wants the juice. I have also seen this baby wrap its arms around my wife's neck, and cry until its face is scarlet, and crawl across the kitchen floor. What a baby.

"So, Alice," says the Colonel, "did your husband tell you

51

about today's tug-of-war?" He knows I haven't. We arrived together, the Colonel and I, and have been in the kitchen with my wife and the baby the entire time. Telling my wife anything that the Colonel didn't hear would have been impossible, and he knows that. But the Colonel is not the kindest man, and he has always been sweet on my wife, and I think he wants to show me up in front of her.

"No, Percy," says my wife. "Am I to assume that Jim had his ass dragged across the line again?" My wife smiles when she says this. She smiles often, actually. All the time. In fact, now that I think about it, I can't honestly remember a single time I've ever seen her with any other expression on her face, even after the cancer turned up, when she was on a chemo routine so powerful it made her hair disappear entirely and then grow back coarse, curly, and reddish. It had always been soft and brown. I moved out to live on base shortly after that. It wasn't her hair that made me go, not only, although I must admit that the last time we talked on the telephone, I imagined that her hair was brown again, and it was harder to forget about her when I put the phone down. My wife is also funny, which is a different thing than this smiling. I mean to say she tells jokes. She used to leave me little notes that had funny parts in them, like "Jim—Went to the moon—will be back in three years. Dinner is in the freezer for you to heat. Love, Alice," when in fact she had just gone to the supermarket or the hardware store. Once at a party, one too many officers tried to buy her a drink or offer her a cigarette. "Goodness, no," she said. "I drink like a chimney and smoke like a fish." One officer laughed, either because of her smile or the joke. He had a light in his eyes the way that men sometimes do. I think it might have even been the General.

In fact, I'm sure it was the General, because later that night we got into a shoving match about it. "You were looking at her all night," I said.

"Which night?" he said. The question threw me for a second, and then he shoved me, and I shoved him back, and we went like that for a little while until the Colonel came outside to separate us. My wife was with him. "Jim," she said, "let's go home. Give me your hand." I did. "You," she said in the car on the way home. "You you you." I didn't know what she meant. That night, she spoke against the General, calling him a boor and an octopus. I found myself defending him. I spoke of his accomplishments in battle and his loyalty to his men, of his enthusiasms for new fashions and his aptitude for numbers. I explained to her why he needed to keep his nose clean. "If you are a woman in the presence of the General," I remember saying, "the kind of man he is needs no explanation." "I don't know what you mean," she said. I told her that it's just a fact that some women can't help but smile at men, make them feel larger and more hopeful, except for the men closest to them, who they make feel small and hopeless. Often these women smile at men in power, who then feel even more powerful. "Some women?" she said. "I could get angry, but I won't."

"What?" I say now to my wife, who is standing by the kitchen sink, emptying the Colonel's untouched glass of tea.

"What what?" she says.

"I thought I heard you call my name," I said.

"Nope," she says.

"Funny," I say. "I could swear."

"I've been sitting here the whole time," says the Colonel, "and I didn't hear anything."

"Jim," my wife says.

"What?" I say.

"What what?" she says.

"Didn't hear a thing," says the Colonel. He scratches his nose.

"Jim," my wife says.

"What?" I say. I could get angry, but I won't. We've been through this before.

"Could you bring me the baby's glass?" She is smiling broadly.

"Sure," I say. "It's right here."

I take the glass from the baby. It's empty. The baby drinks everything, and eats everything, and grabs everything. At the sink, I put the glass in the bottom of the basin, next to a knife and a half-eaten fruit I cannot immediately identify. The Colonel is telling my wife about maneuvers, and how important it is to get them right the first time. "There's no room for error," he says. "You get it wrong once, and you get it wrong forever. That's what the General always says."

"Well, he would know," my wife says. "He's quite an expert at this kind of thing. He's a prince among men. He's the guy that all the other guys want to be. Right, Jim?" I don't answer her. I brush my hand across the baby's mouth. I want the baby to smile. The baby doesn't smile. Instead, it makes a tiny fist around my index finger. The baby has a light in its eyes the way I sometimes did when I was a baby, the way I did when I was a younger man. "Right, Jim?" my wife says again. "Hey," she says. "You know what? Sometimes I get the feeling you're not listening to me." Out of the corner of my eye, I see her take the knife from the table, the one she used to cut the celery. She grasps the handle tight in her right hand, raises it over her head, and then jabs the blade toward me in short, sharp strokes. I don't turn around. I'm trying to make the baby smile. "You know I'm just joking," she says. The Colonel laughs. I can feel my wife's smile at my back. I lower my head to the baby's head, which is warm, and smells faintly of juice. I pull. The baby pulls. What a baby.

VII. Getting Nearer to Nearism

Editor's Note:

In this first half of the book, I have chosen to annotate sparingly, and even this sometimes feels excessive. As a result, after the midword, I will endeavor to disappear completely and let the contents of the book settle inside readers like a large repast. Prose like this must be digested slowly, like any work of art. Let me illustrate my point with an example: The first time you visit Bernini's statue of St. Teresa of Avila in the Cornaro chapel in Rome, you may notice her curled toes, and how they create a sense of spiritual and sensual urgency. But it may take until the second or third visit to illuminate equally important details, such as the saint's right hand, which seems to be at once expressing pleasure and entreating an inexpressible pain to cease. I must confess that I myself did not notice the hand until my fourth viewing, when it was pointed out to me by my traveling companion, who then trotted off to buy more film, and left me there, alone, forsaken, transfixed. While it would be irresponsible for me to compare this book to Bernini's masterpiece, it would be equally irresponsible to ignore the fact that the two works share a type of formal ambition. Bernini combined sculpture, painting, and architecture. Mr. Greenman combines humor, short fiction, and, indeed, architecture, though it is the architecture of syntax and symbol rather than that of marble.

I should also note that this is the first of a set of pieces in this book to employ an Italian setting. Let me be clear about this: whenever Mr. Greenman removes a story to Italy (or, for that matter, Russia), he is writing closer to home than at any other time. Just as the Muscovy inventor of "Snapshot" served as a kind of creative doppelganger, here the Italian artist Paolo Legno helps to reflect Mr. Greenman's concerns about which ideas originate in an artist and which are borrowed from the world around him. And if ideas are borrowed, so are identities: the names in this piece are themselves a kind of house of mirrors, as Paolo Legno, Paul Wood, Pablo Madera, and Inek Drzewo are all the same appellation in different languages, all permutations of the Christian name *Paul* and the surname/common noun *Wood*.

One final note, then on to my midword and afterword, and then I will trouble the reader no more: Just as "Theft of a Knife" uses a second layer of editorial intervention to encode a message to me, this story does as well. In the earlier case, the connection was, admittedly, somewhat tenuous—I was depending upon Mr. Greenman's recollection of an anecdote I related in class a decade ago. Here, the tie that binds is considerably shorter: what is "Legno" but "Onge, L." backwards? Now you begin to see why this book is to be reckoned with, and why I am implicated in its complication.

∿

Among artists, originality and talent are prized above all other qualities, so much so that it is rare to find a renowned artist whose work has an absence of original vision. It is even rarer to find a renowned artist whose work shows no sign of artistic talent or temperament—whose work is, in a way, defiantly artless. Paolo Legno was one of those artists.

The Parma-born, Rome-raised Legno spent his career producing works that can broadly be classified as prints, but which are more accurately described as copies: slightly altered replicas of previously published documents. Legno's works were neither satires nor appropriations. Rather, they were exact-size imitations that differed from the originals only slightly. Legno's first work, Menus, *were near-copies of Roman restaurant menus in which he changed only the prices of the entrees, and only minimally. After* Menus, *he applied the same technique to street maps, tourist pamphlets, liner notes from record albums, and advertising circulars. Over the years, Legno was called a fraud, a genius, and "a Xerox machine with an impish sense of humor"; wary of being classified with Dada, surrealism, conceptual art, or*

media art, Legno coined a term for his own genre, "nearism,"
and promptly became the world's premier nearist. One afternoon
last spring, shortly after the opening of Phone Book, *a show that*
exhibited replicas of sections of the telephone directory, he sat
down with the English painter and critic Paul Wood, a longtime
friend, to discuss his career.

∾

Paul Wood: Let's talk about your new work.

Paolo Legno: *White Pages* or *Yellow Pages*?

PW: Let's start with *Yellow Pages.* They are a series of sheets,
eight in all, that look as if they have been simply ripped out from
a big-city phone book. One is taken from the locksmith section,
one from "Plumbing," one from "Sporting Goods: Retail," and so
on.

PL: Yes.

PW: But these are not actual pages from an actual phone book.

PL: Well, they are partly actual. In *Air-Conditioning: Repair,* for
example, I only altered the names of four repair companies and
then the phone numbers of four different companies. I left the
layout of the page, and the artwork, exactly as it was in the original version.

PW: So if I were to call these phone numbers, I would not reach
air-conditioning repairmen?

PL: You might. Remember, I did not change them all. It is possible that you might select one in which the name and the number
are as they were in the original.

PW: Tell me a little bit about your process. Do you create these works by hand?

PL: I use the same process as the people who created the originals. I design electronic files in a desktop publishing program, and then I output them to the same kind of paper. In the case of "Yellow Pages," I used the same commercial printer.

PW: So how are your works different from the originals?

PL: Slightly. And at the same time, entirely.

PW: What is the point of this exercise? Is it like Borges's Pierre Menard, who exactly rewrote sections of Cervantes's *Don Quixote*?

PL: No. It's not, really. Menard is an interesting case, but not the same case as me, because the original Quixote required an astounding amount of creative energy, and the second Quixote required considerably less. I use originals that required little or no creative energy, and I expend some creative energy in copying them, in that I must invent new names or words or numbers. Borges is writing about a man who is, arguably, less creative than his sources. I am, inarguably, more creative than mine. Should that not give me some measure of satisfaction?

PW: You have said that you are simply making explicit the debts that are implicit in every artwork.

PL: Every artist has sources. Picasso drew on African art. Rauschenberg looked at Johns. When I first started my career as an artist, I was a painter, and I was utterly indebted to Hockney, enslaved to painting works that had a brilliance of hue that concealed the banality of their subject. It was difficult to liberate myself from that. It took great effort, and almost cost me my creative life. Having unshackled myself, I was free to do whatever I wanted.

PW: But drawing stylistic inspiration from another piece of art is somewhat different from borrowing large amounts of another piece of non-artistic printing.

PL: The cardinal rule of this sort of thing is that the cardinal rule is an ordinal rule. What is first is first. Everything else is not-first: second, third, fourth; these are secondary distinctions, but not-first is the primary one. We have the original, and we have the others.

PW: You could say that about any artistic representation. We have life, and then we have art. We have fact, and then we have fiction.

PL: Yes. But I like to think of my work as fact.

PW: Well, even nonfiction is a representation of sorts. That's why we have literary nonfiction.

PL: Not literary nonfiction, though. Fact. As far as I am concerned, my works are entirely factual.

PW: Meaning that they are entirely true? But you know that they are not true, because you have changed information. The price of an item according to one of your *Grocery Store Specials* is not actually the price. The time a movie is showing according to one of your *Movie Times* is not actually the time. You know that because you have read the actual information, and then changed it.

PL: Is a fact that which is indisputably true or is a fact that which assumes the stance of truthfulness?

PW: Is that a rhetorical question?

PL: No.

PW: Okay. Let's talk about counterfeiting. Do you consider your-self a kind of counterfeiter or forger?

PL: I suppose so. But the great forgers work hard to mimic the style of the works they are copying, whether it's currency or Matisse. I do not work hard. It is easy. Because the work is without style. No, that's not right: not without style but without difficult style. It has an easy style: a certain kind of paper, a certain font, a certain piece of clip art. Simple colors. Simple arrangement. This is what I was saying before about the relative difficulty of these works. It is much more difficult to forge the Mona Lisa than to forge a poster promising specials on Granny Smith apples. The Mona Lisa forger might give himself away by not exactly capturing the eye of the original. I could create a verisimilar poster with ease, but I choose to change it slightly: maybe these apples are 99¢ per pound rather than $1.09 per pound.

PW: Does your work, after it is created, become its own original?

PL: Of course. And I will tell you something. I had a student a few years ago who decided to make artworks that stood in relation to my works as my works stand in relation to, say, the public telephone directory or the newspaper ads. He took my work and he created his own electronic file, and he changed a few more things, and he printed them, and he showed them as his own.

PW: Did he get an A?

PL: He did. He was a clever student. But he started me thinking about this, and since then, I have been working on my own second-generation works, in which I work off of my own copies and change the information again.

PW: So you have a work that is even more distant from the original?

PL: That's what is interesting. The second set of changes has, for some reason, been exactly counterweighting the first set of changes. So the second generation copy ends up being exactly the same as the original.

PW: So will these be your next works?

PL: I am thinking about exhibiting my second-generation copies alongside the originals. They are distant cousins who are also identical twins. The slight alteration of my slight alteration is myself. Or else I may exhibit a different set of pieces that I have recently begun. They are catalogs from past shows, and I have collected them, and reprinted them. I am thinking about binding them into a book.

PW: And they just have a few details changed?

PL: No. When it came to the catalogs, I changed almost everything. It is the incontinent version of the controlled experiment I have been performing for the last decade, and it is an exciting departure. I tell you, it is incredibly liberating to be able to change your name, the titles of your works, the dimensions of them, everything but the pictures. I have recreated a version of my restaurant menus where the works exhibited are, according to the notation in the catalog, twenty feet tall. Can you imagine these monumental menus? You would need a waiter more than a hundred feet tall just to carry them to your table.

∼

Soon after the opening of White Pages/Yellow Pages, *the Spanish collector Pablo Madera invited Legno to speak at a symposium in Barcelona. Legno agreed. When he did not appear as sched-*

uled and would not answer his phone, Madera had police enter Legno's hotel room. They found the artist in his bathroom, dead by his own hand. "Those who take their own lives," he once wrote in a letter to the Polish critic Inek Drzewo, "should go by pills, because pills are painless and free of mess, and because they have a printed label that lends itself quite nicely to nearism in a way that other instruments of oblivion, whether gun, rope, or automobile, do not." Legno was perverse even in death. He did not use pills, but rather a pistol, and the fatal course he plotted was hardly free of mess—the officer who discovered his body said that the scene was "like a painting made with blood." To the pistol, Legno had taped a small label on which he had typed the word "gun."

VIII. Marlon Brando's Dreaming

To the door of my modest country home in the placid British town of S., there arrived a package—a nondescript box of the sort favored by online retailers, department stores, catalog houses, shops that line the main streets of S., and, in short, all business who concern themselves with the sale and delivery of goods. In the box was scattered a load of styrofoam peanuts—or rather, I thought that they were styrofoam, and did not consider until later the possibility that they might have been those starch packing peanuts that dissolve in water and can therefore be eaten in large quantities as a means of shocking friends and acquaintances. In addition, there was a blue bottle that, while not large, was not small either. Also, while not ornate, it was not plain. It had no label, even when I turned it around. I searched through the foam peanuts for a card or a packing-slip, but found none. I called my lady friend, whose name eluded me at that moment, to see if she could find any information as to the package's origin, but she was not around. She had, since earlier in the day, been outside with the gardener, huddled in counsel over the fate of the peonies. Then I grew bored, and placing the bottle on top of the dresser by the front door, went upstairs to the bedroom, where I fell into a deep sleep that took the shape of a dream of intensely aerobic carnal congress with a certain starlet of the forties whose films, I am sorry to say, were far inferior to her physical charms. During the night the bottle fell but did not break. My lady friend—by then I had remembered her name, which was

Taluwa—did not join me in my bedroom, but rather slept in her own, and my sleep was rich and rewarding. Coming down for my customary breakfast of eggs and loaves of bread, I noticed it on the floor by the stairs, where it had rolled after its plunge from the dresser. I called for Taluwa again, and this time she answered, but only to tell me that she was still working with the gardener, not on the peonies any longer but on the particularly knotty problem of a potted palm. To my ears, her voice carried, in addition to its usual seductive cast, a tinge of impatience. Ever since I brought her here from the island of Ponape in the eastern Caroline Islands, she has often been short-tempered with me, sometimes inappropriately. I took a nap during breakfast, and another one just after breakfast, and then I picked the bottle up and placed it back on the dresser.

When I awoke from my after-breakfast nap, it was because the gardener, a little man who favored large sweaters, had entered the house. I thought that he was Jewish, although I had never known a Jewish gardener. I thought this only because when I asked him if he would like to join me in a brandy, he declined. Jews aren't big drinkers. Also, once about six months previous, I was typing up a letter to the *New York Times* that discussed the wonderful tendency of the Jew to engage in spirited verbal banter, and the gardener wandered by my desk and fixed me with a look of what I took to be silent disapproval, I assumed ironically. That day, the gardener picked up the bottle, then disappeared upstairs to Taluwa's bedroom to collect something. When he emerged again, he had in his hands what he wished me to think was the same bottle, but what I saw upon closer inspection was an entirely different bottle, narrower at the top, wider at the bottom, and of a hue that tended more toward periwinkle than toward cobalt. As soon as he was outside, I smashed this impostor-bottle into a thousand pieces, then ate some old lasagna I found hiding in the back of the refrigerator. The sauce, once red, had turned a brownish color that I can only describe as "brown-red." If there is a more precise term for this hue, I must confess that I do not know it.

My intent after eating the lasagna was to march right into Taluwa's bedroom and look for the original bottle, after which I would replace it on the dresser where it belonged. But while I was still wiping the last drabs of tomato sauce from my neck, I suffered a dizzy spell that swiftly did away with any thought of ascending the stairs. My episodes, as Taluwa likes to call them, began about ten years ago as infrequent nuisances. Today, they are so common that I cannot often distinguish them from their absence. When they come upon me, my mind melts into a muddle. In *The Island of Dr. Moreau*, a film I consider to be my greatest accomplishment, I wrote much of my own dialogue, including the film's greatest line of dialogue, which also happens to be the greatest line of dialogue ever spoken in the history of cinema: "I have seen the devil in my microscope, and I have chained him." Were I to remake that film, and it is entirely possible that I might, I would rewrite the greatest line of dialogue ever spoken in the history of cinema to make it even greater. "I have seen the devil in my mind," I would say, "and I have claimed him."

But my dizzy spell has distracted the course of my tale. After dashing the blue bottle to pieces, I thought that I was done with the saga of the mysterious vessel. I could not have been more wrong. When I broke it, I noticed a slight smell of sulfur, but did not think anything of it. But when I was eating the wienerschnitzel, which followed the lasagna, I was overpowered by another smell, that of roses. I thought for certain that the scent was somehow connected to the gardener, but neither he nor Taluwa were anywhere to be found. And when I undertook to locate the source of the perfume, I traced it to the spatter of blue glass. I stood over the remnants of the bottle, and then it came to me: the contents of the bottle, first sulfurous and then with the aroma of roses, were the contents of my soul, which had been regrettably demonic when I was a young ruffian but had blossomed into floral enlightenment late in life. Before my eyes, as if responding to my spark of inner vision, the pieces began to reassemble themselves into a whole bottle, and not just any bottle, but the very same bottle that I had received in the mail, the very same bottle that the Jewish gardener had spirited upstairs. I quaked with fear. My knees clapped against one another. I almost dropped the fudgsicle that I clutched with my right hand.

I have not always been receptive to the supernatural. When I first arrived in New York City to study acting, I was, as I have said, willful and reckless, and hardly heeded the laws of man, let alone those of the heavens. But with age, I have learned to read my surroundings for traces of the divine—not just tea leaves and crop circles, but less well-known sources of augury, like the bottom of a rapidly ingested gallon tub of vanilla ice cream. This particular tub, to which I fled after the bottle's resurrection, had a faint yellow streak that brought to mind butter, which in turn brought to mind joy. Suddenly, I felt a stabbing pain in the lower left quadrant of my belly. I palpated there but could find nothing. It seared for a few excruciating seconds, then went as quickly as it had come, leaving behind a newly minted relief. I walked into the living room, where the wicker rocker in the corner beckoned me. I fell into its embrace, and then into the outstretched arms of sleep. The starlet who had visited my dream the night before was there again, this time sitting by herself on a red sofa, investigating herself in a manner that has not been shown on the silver screen since the days before the Hays Code. Flushing with embarrassment and pleasure both, feeling my age, I knelt at her feet, knees creaking loudly, and prayed for her to save me

IX. SOMETREE/ANYTREE?

Say I am a tree and there is another tree next to me. We don't talk at first. That's how trees are: cautious.

But then one afternoon it's nice in the forest, not too warm, not too cold, squirrels and birds present in plentiful but hardly worrisome numbers, and I decide to say hello, and the other tree says hello in return, and that's when it begins.

That first day, it's a long conversation. Have you ever noticed the way the wind comes through here at night? Why are there so many kinds of airborne seeds? Isn't bark weird? By the end of that conversation, I'm pretty sure that the other tree is not just an interesting and intelligent tree, but a fascinating tree, a lovely tree, a wonderful and great tree, one of the best trees I have ever had the pleasure of meeting. I am thrilled to have the other tree next to me, and a little bit embarrassed that I didn't notice the other tree until now. Sometimes those things escape you: there is a sheet of sky to look at, and the purling of a nearby stream.

The next day the other tree and I talk again, all day long, and it's as if that second day, too, is the first day. Every bit of the discussion shines like a particularly smooth, flat stone after a rainstorm.

But it's not nearly as beautiful as the other tree, which I realize the third day, which is spent primarily in contemplation of the tree's charms. Sometimes a trunk is just a trunk, and branches are just branches, but sometimes a trunk has a perfect thickness, and branches taper just right, and then there are the leaves, so exquisitely arranged along each branchlet, with such lovely fall coloration, that it makes me want to hire someone to come out with an axe and chop me down so I can fall near the roots of the other tree and lay there forever. This is the romantic fantasy that I entertain as I talk to the other tree that third day. My conversation is somewhat distracted, but I come out of my fog long enough to see that the other tree's conversation is distracted as well, and that's when it occurs to me that maybe the other tree, too, is dreaming of being chopped down and falling near my roots and lying there forever.

The fourth day I discover that I have a tiny wirelike twig that reaches almost to one of the other tree's twigs, and I concentrate on growing that twig, and while the fifth day is frustrating, the sixth day is far less so, and the seventh and the eighth days are spent in bliss, twigs entwined. "Or is it entwigged?" the other tree says, and this strikes me as the one of the most appealing things I have ever heard, witty and poignant and critical and bewitching all at the same time.

The morning of the ninth day we discover that we're entwigged at a second point, this one a bit closer to the trunk.

The tenth day the other tree loses some leaves, and I offer comforting words, and even point out that a few of my own leaves are falling, that it's a natural process, happens every year, nothing to worry about. The other tree doesn't say anything, but there's a small reward in the form of pressure at that first entwigging point, and that's enough for me.

The eleventh day is like the twelfth, and the thirteenth, and the fourteenth, and the fifteenth. I only know that time is passing because the sun rises and sets.

Then, on the sixteenth day, I notice something strange. A few of the knots of twigs have undone themselves. I ask the other tree about it, and the answer is vague, something about cold air coming up from the other side of the forest. This isn't how it works with twigs, and I know it, and I know that the other tree knows it, but I don't make a big deal about it.

The seventeenth day, more entwiggings disappear, and on the eighteenth, only the original one is left.

By now, I can't keep quiet any longer, and I ask the other tree a series of questions, trying to keep my tone level and calm but, I'm sure, betraying my anxiety and anger and desire and, above all, my sadness. That's when the other tree tries to fend me off with a metaphor. Assume, the other tree says, that there are two trees next to one another, and they grew closer, sometimes by almost imperceptible degrees. But then assume that there is a countermovement, and they grow more distant, sometimes by almost imperceptible degrees. It doesn't mean that the trees are less beautiful to one another, or even less close to one another. It is difficult to move a trunk. It just means that sometimes twigs will do what twigs will do. "There are other trees on the other side of me," the other tree says. "They have twigs, too." I explain that I don't care about that, and at that moment I don't. Trees have hundreds of twigs. I know that. I'm not an idiot. I just know what I like—what I need—and that's the feeling of some of the other tree's twigs entwined with my twigs. The other tree tells me I'm yelling, and I realize I am, and that's when I go dead silent.

The nineteenth day is a wintry day, the first really unpleasant weather of the year, and I spend most of the morning feeling one of my own leaves working itself free from a branch. Finally a small blast of icy wind dislodges it, and it falls, slowly, with a side-to-side motion, and for a moment it looks as if the leaf might come to rest on one of the other tree's branches before sliding off and disappearing against the carpet of leaves, the gold, the red, the orange, the brown. I want the leaf to brush across the other tree's branch on its way down, to serve as a reminder, if only for a moment, of the feeling of twig on twig. I don't want the other tree to feel guilty. It's only the fact of my devotion that I want the other tree to feel, and not even all of it, just a bit of it, which is powerful, which is enough. But to feel the fact of a devotion that is, for the moment, detained. This is a form of melancholy, much like the fact that a leaf will fall and lay motionless before sinking into the earth and disappearing forever. The leaf bounces on an updraft. I look away.

The twentieth day I stop looking away. Who has time for petulance? The other tree is just as lovely as ever. The way the lowest, largest branches flow out of the trunk breaks my heart.

MIDWORD

By Laurence Onge

First off, let me take credit where credit is due. I coined the word "midword." Etymologically, it is easy to see how: I took the word "word" and affixed the prefix "mid," which can mean "in the middle of," as in midtown (in the middle of town) or mid-century (in the middle of the century). But "mid" can also have another meaning in which mid-x delineates an x surrounded by other x's that both precede and follow, either spatially or temporally. The clearest example that springs to mind is "midsection": this is not some zone in the middle of a previously existing "section" but rather a section between two other sections. Also: mid-sole. The word "middle" itself is a mystery. I do not know its history. It rhymes with "riddle," which should be cause enough to leave it alone. One moment: telephone.

Where was I? Ah, yes. Midword. So this is a word in the middle of other words. Here, of course, "word" does not mean one word but rather a set of words, just as "duck" does not always mean one duck but rather a set of ducks. I belabor these rather niggling issues only because I want each and every reader to understand precisely how this midword functions with relation to Mr. Greenman's Superworse. It is not, like the foreword, before the book. It is not, like the afterword, after the book. It is here, in the middle. I could have called it "Midbook," but that sounds like an unfortunate contraction of "Middlebrook," which is itself an unfortunate translation of "Buddenbrooks."

I am not the only one who has taken such care with the par-

71

ticulars of text. I have explained how the original Superbad, *the hardback precursor to* Superworse, *was intended as a perfectly balanced and calibrated structure. But it was written in the early morning of Mr. Greenman's intellect, in the hours before the dawn, when a mist still hung over the ground like a shroud. Now, with my help—I stood in for the sun—the haze has been burned off and the work's scheme, burnished and tightened, can be exposed. The first step in this process is to show you where you are: to reveal, in short, that you are standing before "Notes to a Paper You Wouldn't Understand," which is not an ordinary text by any standard but rather an answer to the question of the rest of* Superworse. *To mix metaphors willfully and gleefully, it is a passe-partout that opens eighteen doors, meaning the eighteen other sections in this book, and then uses those eighteen doors as keys to a much larger door, the overarching work itself. (This was obscured slightly in the original book by the inclusion of a number of celebrity musicals. I was the one who wanted them in. I now concede that they were tonally disruptive, though I still hold that they are among the most trenchant pieces of literature written in the post-War era, assuming that we are speaking of the first Gulf War, and that Mr. Greenman should never have turned his attentions from them. Unfortunately, authorial pressure, and even a tinge of fury, has forced me to marginalize my enthusiasm. [See Appendix, page 153.])*

The nineteen footnotes that make up "Notes to a Paper You Wouldn't Understand" relate, in severely elliptical style, the story of an author named George Vinton, who began his career as a poet (footnote 1), and later became a mystery novelist (3). Along the way, he married a woman named Molly Grange (2) and did battle with a critic named Howard Salter (13, 19), but his most important intimacy seems to be his relationship with an older author and critic named Kenneth Burnham (1, 5, 10, 12, 14, 15, 19). The notion of a bond between mentor and protégé dates back to the nineteenth century, and possibly beyond. As long as there have been ambitious and talented young men whose lack of experience prevented them from taking a measure of their own creative endowment, there have been patient older men willing to take hold of that endowment and guide it to a satisfactory conclusion. But the investigation of the Vinton–Burnham relationship is also, I believe, a coded message from Mr. Greenman intended to alert me to the importance of my own mentorship in his life. There is ample evidence of this, some of which I have already mentioned (the disinterment of the story of Carl Jung's flatware in "The Theft of the Knife," the inversion of my name to create the name Legno in "Getting Nearer to Nearism").

The most compelling evidence resides in the story you are about to read, "Notes to a Paper You Wouldn't Understand." This is where I pull back the curtain and expose the great and powerful Oz. To reiterate, there are nineteen footnotes in "Notes to a Paper You Wouldn't Understand," and nineteen stories in Superworse*; furthermore, the footnotes are mapped precisely onto the stories. For example, the first footnote corresponds to the first story, "Ill in '99," and both texts deal explicitly with career crisis and mentorship—Vinton is encouraged to switch from poetry to prose by the critic Umberto Gettlioni, and the protagonist of "Ill in '99" has a more fraught encounter with a graying barfly named Tom Lehman. The third footnote explicitly recreates the central problem of "Snapshot"—what happens, metaphysically speaking, when a man is photographed at the moment of his death. Each footnote, in other words, distills and amplifies the themes of its partner story. At times the intertextual connections are quite straightforward: In the eighth footnotes, the names of the authors cited, Malloy and Diestl, correspond to characters played by Marlon Brando (the protagonist of the partner story) in* On the Waterfront *and* The Young Lions, *respectively. At other times the links are more reticulate. The seventh footnote, for instance, contains the same play of real and unreal, actual artist and manufactured artist, as the seventh chapter, "Getting Nearer to Nearism," but also subtly inverts its terms—the two artists that Vinton "manufactures," Mary Anfinsen and Boyce Day, are of course quite real in our world.*

That is the first of the book's structural secrets. The second

relates to the fact that this is a midword. Why a midword?
Because Superworse, *the entire book, is constructed with an eye*
toward perfect symmetry. Not only are footnotes mapped onto
stories, but stories are mapped onto one another. Imagine the
book's contents laid out on a long strip of paper which is then
folded in half lengthwise. The result would be a kind of hinged
structure in which each story had a twin equidistant from the
book's midpoint. The first and last chapters both deal with the
deaths of loved ones. The second and the penultimate are both
short conceptual jottings. The third and the antepenultimate are
Russian stories; and so forth. This perfectly symmetrical struc-
ture, taken in conjunction with the footnote-to-story mapping,
not only intensifies the notion of correspondence but focuses a
sharp spotlight on the only point that cannot be truly reflected by
a mirror—the midpoint. The midpoint is the tenth section, of
course: this next story. It stands alone: the rest of Superworse
rotates around it. Similarly, the tenth footnote is a kind of ful-
crum. In this paragraph of a mere 275 words, the book's true
meaning is revealed—the Paper that Would Not Be Understood,
you see, is in fact Superworse. *Now, I am wary of overdetermin-*
ing the text and doing readers' job for them, but it seems clear to
me what has happened. In the fiction, after Burnham helps
Vinton with his work, Vinton spurns Burnham, who eventually
dies of a broken heart. The protégé rejects the mentor and, while
only one man suffers on the face of it, both men suffer in their
hearts. It seems, to be blunt, like one long apology to me.

Let us not be confused. I would like nothing better than to be
utterly unimplicated. But that would be a form of blindness, and
while it may not surprise you that Mr. Greenman has written a
book that conceals a message to me, it may surprise you to learn
that it has been years in the making. A few months before com-
ing here to New York from Chicago, I was cleaning out my attic
and found a number of old stories by students, one of which was
Mr. Greenman's. That story, which was titled "The Spider in the
Skirt," opened with a snippet of verse written by the book's pro-
tagonist. I share it with you in the hopes that you will under-

stand the depth of mechanism at work here.

Ten is a sign of finding, the X that marks the spot.
It is the reel, winding. It is the clue, still hot.

This is substandard doggerel, but consider its context: in that story, a young writer named Benson finds a treasure buried in the back yard of his neighbor, an older man named Lawrence. All those years ago, Mr. Greenman was already directing me to look here, at the tenth story, at the tenth footnote, where I would be paid my proper respects. I take this verse now as I could not before, as a tribute: indeed, I take the entire novel as a tribute. I hope that I am not the only one to benefit from this clarification. So much of the book's meaning has run out of the open wounds of misunderstanding and indifference. I hope that knowledge of the schematic can serve as a kind of ischemy. Now I will trouble you no more. Having sent the boats from the harbor, I wish only for light winds and mare liberum.

X. Notes to a Paper You
Wouldn't Understand

1. In the fifties, Vinton was still entirely defined by his association with the Enjoin movement: see Randolph Descombes, "The Enjoin Poets Make Less With More Language"; Francis Embry, "What Goes Down Must Come Up"; and a volume jointly edited by Descombes and Embry entitled *Desire Cannot Be Contained.* The last of these is of special interest, since it contains the essay in which Umberto Gettlioni suggested that Vinton try his hand at writing prose. "There is one among them," he wrote, "who has thus far labored, in my mind, in the wrong mine. I mean, of course, George Vinton, whose work has shown the least promise of any of the first wave of Enjoin poets. Vinton's problem, I believe, is not one of incompetence, but rather of dislocation. Were he to write a series of short stories or a novel, I feel we might see a different man."(99) Kenneth Burnham was shown the essay by Michelangelo Gettlioni, Umberto's nephew, and mentioned it to Vinton in a letter. "Dear boy," he wrote, "some addlepated critic has come up with a preposterous notion that your talents should be wasted telling stories."

2. Weeks before his first motorcycle accident, Vinton had what he called an "insultingly, transparently prophetic dream." In a journal entry of June 8, 1958, he wrote, "Motorcycle crashing. Could not see face of man riding cycle, but believe that it was me from name tag on jacket that read 'G. Vinton.'" The journal entry is also noteworthy in that it contains the first mention of Molly

Grange, who was introduced to Vinton at a party and stuck in his mind as a result of her "red hair and shoes."

3. Zeno's Paradox, of course, is the age-old mathematical/philosophical conundrum that holds that it is impossible to travel from point A to point B, because travel can be expressed as a infinite series of halvings of the interval distance. Xeno's Paradox, less well known, was posed by the early-twentieth-century British writer, Geoffrey Stanhope, who adopted the Greek *nom de plume* as a tribute to his forbears, and it concerns the problem of artistic representation. "Is a picture more or less real than the object it depicts?" Stanhope wrote. "If a dying man sits for a portrait, and then expires, and his picture persists, who is to say that it is not more real than the man, or more real than he had ever been?" Vinton recommended Stanhope's work to Molly Grange, and during a vacation they took to Capri in 1961, he gave her a copy. In return, she gave Vinton a copy of Hammett's *The Continental Op*, a decision, of course, that proved immensely influential.

4. Though many of Kubelick's poems from this period were titled as if they were light verse, they were in fact his most serious works. Vinton seems to have followed this lead for "False Starts, False Hearts" and "I Wrote You a Note on the Boat."

5. Few have remarked upon the fact that it was his second visit to Brisbane. The first, five years earlier, had been in the company of Burnham, and it was under the older man's influence that Vinton wrote the vast majority of "A Grand and Hopeful Plan." With Short, Vinton sketched out the plot for his first mystery novel, *The Damned Shame of Louis Soule*. Burnham was heartbroken when he heard of Vinton's plans: "There is no pain sharper than this news," he wrote.

6. Petty's name, of course, dervies from that of Marcus Petty, who served with Vinton in Korea. But the fact that he was a real man does not mean that the choice is not significant. Some crit-

ics have even suggested that Mark Petty's name is a pun of sorts, Vinton's attempt to encode his equivocal feelings about the written word. Lance Warner's "Evasive Action" is a good general study of what he calls "self-seditious literature." See also A. Childs, "When Is A Whodunit Not a Whodunit? Mysteries as Master-Texts."

7. "Need title for new book," he wrote to Grange as he labored to produce a sequel to *The Damned Shame of Louis Soule.* "Working title is 'Working Title,' but I'm not happy with that. Also considering 'Not Happy with This,' which seems slightly better." A week later, another letter follows: "Despair all gone— solved it while reading the poetry of Mary Anfinsen and listening to the songs of Boyce Day." It is typical of him to locate his inspiration in the works of others. Interestingly, there is no record of either of them existing. Perhaps they were manufactured by Vinton.

8. Diestl and Malloy have addressed this issue in the monograph, *Stabbing Pains: The Social Significance of Cutlery in the British Murder Novel.*

9. "'Touch, tip, shatter, repair, touch, tip, shatter, repair, touch, tip, shatter, repair, touch, tip, shatter, repair.' It's a beautiful line, granted, but now I'm out four vases." (11) Vinton's "What is Left of Her Lips" was a return to his poetry.

10. Though *The Raw Deal of Walter Brown* would prove to be even more successful than *The Lost Cause of Arthur Cross,* Vinton had great doubts about the work. In fact, he wrote Burnham a letter listing nineteen reasons why he feared the book would be a failure, including: "Because readers will not see that the mystery is constructed with perfect symmetry," "Because readers will be displeased by the seemingly random relationship between short chapters and long chapters," and "Because Mark Petty never does anything. Sits, thinks, sits thinks, sits." "Still,"

he wrote, "there is an answer, and it sits at the dead center of the novel, and I believe that those who find it deserve their reward entirely." Burnham's response disappointed him. He claimed credit for much of Vinton's career, and Vinton, in return, broke off with him. Burnham's response was all out of proportion. He fired off a number of letters, made at least one profane phone call (Grange answered the phone), and published a scathing attack on the "school of fizz, or is it fizzle" that derided Vinton as a vacant stylist. See V. Petrancko, "Mentorship as A Form of Displaced Narcissism" (Chicago, 1974) for a full account of the events. Vinton's next novel, *The Broken Spirit of Fredrick Furst,* was likely intended as a counterattack: the titular Furst is an aging painter who is murdered by a young musician. Over a matter of months, Vinton relinquished his grudge against Burnham. "It is an act of economic mercy," he said, according to a letter Grange wrote to her friend Henry Shell. "It means so much to him and so little to me."

11. A similar thesis has been developed by L.T. Honegger: see *The Locus Of Location: A Brief Consideration of the Topographical Psychology ("Boekbesprekingen") of Anthropomorphism.*

12. Burnham briefly became preoccupied with the work of Madame Cicisbeo, a late nineteenth-century medium who developed the pseudoscience of "dorsology"—it functioned like phrenology, but posited that a man's character could be judged by looking at his back. Vinton replied with typical malapertness: "Dorsology my ass."

13. It is unquestionable that Howard Salter's famous critique of *The Raw Deal of Walter Brown* incorporated the material from Vinton's letter to Burnham. Vinton, who had not known about the sexual relationship between Salter and Burnham, was perplexed at first, and then furious. "I wish I had sent you a puffed-up, preening bit of self-congratulatory nonsense," he wrote.

"Then maybe Salter would have written a good review. He does not seem to think for himself."

14. The most flagrant of the psychoanalytic critics is indisputably Marjorie Leacock: "Burnham was ashamed of his own ailment, but also angry at Vinton for what he perceived as a betrayal. Consider the letter of July 9, 1968, in which Burnham objects to Vinton's decision to travel out West without him. In that letter, Burnham complains bitterly that Vinton is driving him to drink, and notes 'You will put me in my grave, though when I am there I will reverse the letters on my gravestone so as to escape simple detection. You will need a mirror to find me.' The tropes of abandonment and inversion are so clear they might as well be in a textbook."

15. Olivares was a Mexican middleweight turned playwright who wrote a series of what he called "metaphysical mysteries." His most famous work was "Celos (Jealousy)," which told the tale of two kings from adjoining lands who dueled one another over the affections of a young woman. The progress of the duel, it should be noted, closely parallels that of Olivares's 1961 title fight against Esteban "Burrito" Padilla.

16. It was this phone call from Grange that led Vinton to write the famous closing lines of *The Rotten Luck of Marvin Eagleton*: "He picked up the dead woman's hand and looked at it for a while. It was a hand like any other hand, and as such did not hold his interest long."

17. Vinton's interest in libraries as sites of crimes is one of the most studied aspects of his oeuvre. See Nicholas Prince, "Metareference in the Library of the Mind" and Albert Haake, "Speaking Volumes."

18. Edward Pochman's "Doing Time" is an excellent study of sequential illogic in Vinton's mysteries.

19. Burnham's death was ruled an accident, although Salter believed otherwise, and said so in a letter to Vinton that he composed but never mailed. It is now part of the Howard Salter Papers at the University of Texas. "Ask anyone who knew him," Salter wrote. "To say that you betrayed him is something of an understatement. Worst of it is that he never meant to hurt you. Ken Burnham was a good man who loved your poems, and who felt that your other work was beneath you. He was honor-bound to say so, and you, my boy, were honor-bound to listen. You did not. You mocked. You lampooned. You lived your life on the Continent, on blood money earned from work that would have been impossible without him. You cannot say that Ken was a villain. At worst, you can accuse him of being a critic; as one myself, I know the full horror of that existence."

IX. REELING

Editor's Note:
As I vowed not to intrude too often into the second half of this book, I will offer two brief comments, only: 1. In a piece of fiction such as this, what is a squirrel but a man dressed as a squirrel? 2. The mitten is an archetypal example of a transitional object, or the first not-me object experienced by a child emerging into consciousness (see Winnicott, "Home is Where We Start From").

They were a family of squirrels, and they were reeling. There were five, two slightly larger than an average squirrel, two slightly smaller than an average squirrel, and one so small it might have been mistaken for a mouse—except of course by squirrels, who always know their own. The five squirrels sat in the shade of a large oak tree, forest caps and flowers at their feet, and while the smallest squirrel was quite animated—he parted the wet grass with his tiny paws and pushed his nose into the dirt, squealing with delight—the rest of the family of squirrels was sad. Sorrowful. Despondent. They were sad because the little one was dead, and the parting of grass and pushing of nose was no more than a dream of what might have been, and not the truth of the matter. How can you speak of a truth of the matter then the matter is squirrels and their sadness? Simple. You look at the crumpled body of the smallest squirrel, you see its eyes gone dull like fogged glass—cold on the inside—you see its fur beginning to drop in tufts from its tail and nape, and you feel the sad pull of truth. Squirrel death is no less real than any other death. With its absence of ceremony, mythology, and sentiment, it is perhaps more real.

A short life is sometimes taken without warning; in a storm, when a cannonade of rain and the noise of blue knives in the sky sends a young squirrel scurrying up an oak, and then the increasing violence of the weather keeps him huddled there, chattering like a baby bird, calling out (to friends? gods?), until the tree itself divides in blinding light. And then the squirrel, scorched in a thin line along his tiny belly, falls to the ground with an odd and understated grace, the wet grass padding the fall, a silence rising off him like smoke from a dying fire. Squirrel, rainstorm, lightning. A trinity that toys with the notion of spirit and then declines.

The largest of the squirrels, a female, walked in a slow circle around the tiny corpse, careful not to disturb its peace. The peace of the dead is so fragile. Then the other adult squirrel, not quite as fat and not quite as brown, rose up on his back legs. A southern wind blew stiffly, dislodging raindrops from the branches above, releasing them from their captivity so that they fell into the grass around the body. The raindrops vanished inside shallow pools of standing water. The fur of the standing squirrel moved like feathers in the wind. The two smaller squirrels brought nuts and acorns and pebbles, and placed them in patterns around the inert body, patterns that reminded them of games played before the coming of the blue knives in the sky. One nut went underneath the dead squirrel's tiny head, like a pillow whose hardness was itself a form of comfort, proof that the hard world does admit a kind of mercy. Of the two squirrels who had collected the nuts and acorns, one retreated from the body, which was beginning to thicken in its joints and face, retreated to a nearby path, where the two larger squirrels were already assembled. The other did not join the group, choosing instead to stand over the tiny squirrel and brush one paw plaintively across its belly, which caught the afternoon sun as it had always caught the afternoon sun, with tiny bursts of light exploding at the tip of every hair.

Each hair had a name, produced a sound, made a hopeful promise that it broke as soon as it was swept inside the shade that moved across the body. Whatever the history of a life, it has in its final moments a kind of power—beyond grace, beyond sense—that demands vigilance, and so the squirrel kept watch over his dead brother. The next day, and the day after that, the body would begin to fall away, to leak into the ground, to sanctify the spot where the smallest squirrel had dreamed about pressing his nose into the dirt. For now, the brother, the survivor, the sentinel, waited until darkness had made the color of the body the same as the color of the grass around it, waited until his own gaze matched that of the tiny corpse, waited until the dream dissolved, and then he turned to reclaim his place among his family. But they were gone.

It doesn't seem fair to follow the living squirrel, the small one who stayed behind to tend to a dead brother. Issues of loyalty, privacy, propriety, and so on. But how can narrative remain fixed upon the dead? Narrative moves—uncertainly sometimes, equivocally always, but inexorably. Time needs another minute, at least. And in that minute, the squirrel, suddenly alone, scurried in the direction he thought his family had gone, toward the city rather than toward the river. He darted through the struts of a bench, skirted an overgrown corner of the park where an aged and feral possum was said to lurk, slipped through ferns, feeling the leaves slicken under his wet nose. In a clearing he saw another squirrel, and flicked his tail to gain speed, but when he drew nearer he discovered no squirrel at all, only a wet paper bag swaddling a gray wool mitten. A button hung off the mitten like an eye. Where was the other? Lost, probably, unless this was the lost one, and the other was zipped safely within a jacket pocket halfway across town. The squirrel paused and stepped into a blue pool that seemed to have leaked from the moon. Upstart light, a form of trespass, and a way of thieving bravery, until something in the night air broke the moonlight and put a shadow upon his back. What was it? A crooked bough? A bird whose wings remade the night? A memory of loss?

A lost mitten is an accident. A lost child is a tragedy. A lost squirrel is an adventure, charged with possibility, moving like a streamer, faintly risible. He pushed on toward the city, looking for a tree to climb, a bit of food to eat. He had no intention of finding his family any longer. In fact, he had already forgotten them, and remembered only the tiny form of his brother, neck crooked at an angle of alarm, an angle of impossibility, a single thin root running out from beneath his head like a trickle of blood. The memory scraped his heart like rough bark sometimes scraped his belly, and the bird overhead—for it was a bird after all—glanced downward as if the rasp were audible. The squirrel paused, listened to his own quick breaths, put a paw experimentally inside his mouth and made an ugly face. Dark trees flowed upward from the ground until they washed out against the bruise blue evening sky.

The night became a dance, flowerbeds and streetlights. Dart in front of dog, scurry over newspaper, never wake a sleeping man. The scent of alcohol rose off one man's boots; scarred by scuff marks, they looked like dead things. How was this man different from the tiny squirrel? He was larger—only that. If his brother had been that large, the squirrel would still be waiting for the sun to ignite the final stretch of fur; would still hope for a divine reprieve. Perhaps it was the tininess that had let him go so easily into death. On a porch, in a garbage can, he found food. Pudding in the porchlight, a half-eaten turkey sandwich squirming in a gray plastic container, bugs lining the yellow edge where the mayonnaise caked. The squirrel ate hungrily, and when he was full, he curled up in a corner of the porch. A blue light buzzed overhead, more brilliant than the moon, with stripes that made a buzzing noise when bugs entered its mesh. He fell asleep in neon glow, the angry drone of dying flies covered by a sweetness in his ear.

He had a dream. Squirrels dream. A dream of holding, and of being held, of curling up alongside a body much like his own, but somehow different. He understood that this was his tiny brother grown. His dream was mostly eyes, his tiny brother's eyes, and the way they shaped to wonder and to joy. He had lagged behind when the other four took brisk walks. He had collected extra acorns, unnecessary food, against the laws of nature. He had been born too close to death. Then he was tiny again. He held one in his mouth, and then swallowed it whole. His body shook, his throat stretched as if it would burst, but the acorn went down and stayed down. The dreaming squirrel could see the contours of the nut inside his brother's belly; the fur along its curve was charred and bristled. When the acorn was down, the tiny squirrel clapped both paws over his mouth, then thrust them violently away in a gesture of announcement. From his open mouth a stream of flies emerged, propelled by fetid breath. One of the flies was a bird.

When the squirrel woke, it was early morning, and the clank of pots inside the house sent him scampering off the porch. At a nearby pond he washed his paws, and then walked across a narrow strip of beach to dry them. The beach had black sand so fine he could not hear his own footfalls in the silt. A pane of glass, nicked at two of his corners, leaned against a tree stump, and he stood on his legs and looked inside it. He knew this was his own reflection, the almond-shaped eyes, the tight brown patch of fur upon the brow, but when he touched a paw to the pane he wasn't sure. He bared his teeth in mock anger, part of a game he used to play with his brother. How do you take a game for two and learn to play with one? You start, and you never stop. The squirrel kept his paw upon the pane, saw a mouse run through the dry grass next to the lake, pushed his paw harder into the reflection. He knew it was his own. If he saw other squirrels, he would account them as large mice. He was lost inside the glass. His own family would mean nothing to him. He was with his brother in his loneliness. He would never understand. He could not miss him any more, or any less.

VIII. Blurbs

Editor's Note:
You have by now seen the delightful dorsology footnote in "Notes to a Paper You Wouldn't Understand," which is intended to remind us that a book cannot be judged by its cover, or for that matter by its back cover. The section was prompted by an idea that first took shape in a postcard Mr. Greenman sent to me: "If I cannot avoid the critics, then why not pre-empt them?" It included one fascinating error: for pre-empt, he typed "pre-empty."

"Devilishly brilliant—a bewitching mix of metafiction and marketing."
—*New York Times*

"In just 400 words, this piece dismantles the history of modern literature and pieces it back together again."
— *Los Angeles Times*

"The central conceit—a humor piece composed entirely of blurbs about that humor piece—reads like a mobius strip tied around Jorge Luis Borges's finger."
—*Boston Globe*

"Every writer dreams of writing his own blurbs. This writer has done that, and only that, and benefitted immensely from it. His sly wit conceals a grand scheme, and the completion of that scheme only intensifies the power of that wit."
—*Washington Post*

"After the first blurb, you'll find yourself confused. After the second, amused. But by the fourth or fifth, you'll find yourself cheering."
—*USA Today*

"Initial bemusement will turn to wonder—this is sophisticated stuff indeed."
—*Kirkus Reviews*

"Imagine a cross between the blurbs from *Bridges of Madison County* and the blurbs from *Infinite Jest.*"
— *Cleveland Plain Dealer*

"Marvelous . . . Bracing . . . A short, sharp work combining myth and romance, social commentary and poetry."
—*Publishers Weekly*

"Blurbs has the advantage of novelty, but it is not simply a novelty. Rather, it is something startling, an entirely new foray into our critical assumptions about literature, both highand low."
—*Houston Chronicle*

"A splendid piece, beautifully conceived and crafted . . . no other collection of blurbs this year comes close."
— *Mercury News* (San Jose)

"If John Barth met Samuel Beckett in a bar, and the two of them got into a cab, and the cab picked up Andy Kaufman, and then the cab driver turned around, and it was Dorothy Parker, that would be awfully strange. It would also be the rough equivalent of this marvelous short work."
—*Baltimore Sun*

"In the traditional humor piece, society is satirized with the help of plot, or characters. "Blurbs" throws that all away, bravely, and what it finds is something much more precious: a purity of comic conception that holds a mirror up to the entire human race."
—*Hartford Courant*

"'Blurbs' demonstrates a fresh talent at play in the fields of his mind. Expert command of the blurb form and a wickedly clever worldview add up to paydirt. Ignore this piece at your own peril!"
—*San Francisco Chronicle*

"Marked by a rare piquancy, this collection of blurbs sneaks up on you, and before you know it, you're in its clutches. This is fascinating comedy, with energy to spare. Bravo!"
—*Chicago Tribune*

VII. No Friend of Mine: Guido Cavalcanti, Florence, 1300

Editor's Note:
As in this piece's twin, "Getting Nearer to Nearism," the use of the Italian setting signifies that things are slightly askew or even unreal. To Mr. Greenman, Italy is a land of fantasy: is that why the character was originally named Calvino? Notice that the story contains another explicit mentor relationship.

He says he is a friend. He is no friend of mine. I have been saying that since I arrived here in Sarzana, to whomever will listen.

I sleep on a thin wooden bed. I take my meals alone. I have no visitors except my memories, and they are jumbled by sadness and by age. Time runs away from me.

My wife, who I have not seen in some months, wrote me a letter in which she confessed her fear that I might be mad: *You seem to forget so many things. I wonder what you remember.* I feel the pressure of this question more pointedly than she does. Since I arrived here in Sarzana, I have resolved to create a record of my past. Starting with a few large sheets of parchment, and then tearing those sheets into smaller pieces, I have jotted down dates, places, anything that might trigger my memory. There are scraps of paper that note first meetings and others that record deaths, scraps that record simple impressions and others that represent complex discussions whose meaning I still, after all these years, cannot fathom. The scraps of paper are stacked at the edge of the table, against the wall. Sometimes I pick up a single scrap and try to summon up the piece of the past to which it corresponds. Sometimes I arrange a set of scraps in order, left to right, on the thin wooden table that runs parallel to my bed. Pieces of paper, laid end to end, in danger of being disarranged by a breeze: That is what passes for time these days.

Just this morning, I recovered another memory, one for which I do not yet have a corresponding scrap of paper. This was a memory of Durante, and how I once chanced upon him sitting on a flat, gray rock. The sky above him echoed the rock. "What is gray," he said, "but black and white in battle, neither able to vanquish the other?" This was in Florence, some fifteen years ago, when he was a young man—when we were both young men—and I could laugh with a light heart and move along, pleased with his wit. I remembered him as a child, remembered how I had thought myself a young man then. I had recognized a brightness in his eyes and befriended him, and we had walked the length of the city sometimes, talking about poetry. We were both students of Brunetto Latini, and we amused each other with imitations of the old man. When I saw him sitting on the rock that morning, I took a step forward and left him at my back. I should have taken a step backward and kept him in my sights. That would have been more circumspect. *Flat gray rock*, I scribble on a strip of paper, and place it on top of the pile.

I pick up another scrap of paper that reads *God made a wretch when he made you,* and turn it over in my hands. On that morning, the sky was bright blue, and the sunlight was loose and wild in the Piazza Santa Maria Novella. I paused to wash my hands in the fountain and then continued on my errand. "Please say that Guido Cavalcanti is here," I told Brunetto Latini's servant.

Brunetto Latini had a jug of wine in his hand when he rose to meet me. It was a surprisingly large vessel, and it must have been heavy, as well, because it tilted Brunetto Latini to one side, lifting his opposite leg off the floor. "Dunce," he said. "Welcome." That's what he called me, although he insisted it was a term of affection. You had to take Brunetto Latini in small bites, or else you would choke. "You do not know how to perform the simplest task," he croaked. "God made a wretch when he made you."

"Can I pour you a glass?" he said, indicating the wine with his chin. I declined. "Only a fool says no to wine," he said. The time with Brunetto Latini had always been like this. When I was a boy, I came to study with him, to learn about poetry and politics, to hear him read selections from the *Tesoretto*. As I grew older, I brought him my own work to read, and he mocked me and called me "dunce" before plunging into the poems with an intensity that approached trance. When he finally lifted his head, he gave me his opinion: the opening stanzas struck him as poor, but the language toward the end was superb; or the wonderful beginning was squandered by impure motives. The older he became, the deeper were his silences, and the more wine was needed to fill them. Finally, there came a time when I did not care to sit and wait.

This particular afternoon, Brunetto Latini asked me to sit. "What do you have for me, dunce?" he said. I told him that I had one new poem. "What is it about, dunce?" I told him that it was about my wife. "Ah," he said. "And do you want to know what I have for you?" I did, and he produced a sheaf of poems that I had brought him a few days previous. The papers were ripped at the corners, and stained along the edges with wine. "Let me recall my thoughts," he said, and bent his head to the page. I studied his face. The skin had grown cracked with age. A pair of bristly hairs protruded from his chin. The tip of his nose drooped so low that it looked as if it might fall into his wine. "Idiot," he said, straightening up suddenly, "to what does a good verse bear greater resemblance? A chalice or a candle?" I didn't like these questions. Even though they sounded philosophical, there was usually one right answer, and the wrong answer would bring his index finger, the boniest of several bony digits, into a position of cocked disapproval. In this case, his age worked to my advantage; he had asked me this question many times before.

"A chalice," I said, "because it yields its secrets when tipped, but keeps its form always."

"Very good," he said. "And yet, this work you have given me is a candle, whose mission is to burn with light and heat both, yes, but until it loses all shape." He picked up the jug. I heard the wine slosh against the bottom. He had enough for at least two more hours, and so I stood to leave.

"Fool!" he said. "Where do you think you are going?"

"For a walk. I will leave the new poem with you."

"And what am I to do?"

"You are to read it."

My tone must have been harder than I intended, for his shoulders slumped. "Goodbye," he said gently. "I will see you tomorrow, then."

~

The scrap of paper goes back onto the stack. I eat some bread and drink some wine and then, with the board of the bed beneath my back, I try to sleep. But my mind will not come across the span of years; stubbornly, it cleaves to the past.

The day had soured while I was in with Brunetto Latini. The sky had lost its blue, and now threatened rain. I did not, however, quicken my step. If anything, I slowed down, took care in placing one foot ahead of the other as I went by the three trees—ash, oak, and poplar—in the Piazza Salvemini. "Two trees together are a suggestion, but three together are an argument," Brunetto Latini was fond of saying. I had recently resolved an argument within myself: after many years of unhappiness with my wife, I had taken a lover. My beloved and I had met on the street many times before we met behind closed doors. Then, one day, I followed my beloved home. Afterwards, we were still only acquaintances when we saw each other in public, no more than polite. We nodded to one another and moved on. My beloved was prized by others, took lovers other than me, concealed the time we spent together through misdirection and lies. I would have denied any involvement if asked. Such things are not uncommon.

At the Piazza Santa Croce, I bounded up a flight of stairs,

went across a narrow hallway, and found myself in the arms of my beloved. We went immediately to the bed, a journey that was not without a moment of comedy: there was a box at the foot of the bed upon which I invariably banged my right foot. It was positioned conspicuously, was a dark wood that stood out in the room, and yet each and every time I managed to trip over it.

"Your silence is transparent," my beloved said afterward, when I was standing by the window, gazing out across the Piazza Santa Croce.

"Silence always is," I said.

"You are thinking of your wife," my beloved said. "You are as divided as Florence." I laughed, because I thought the remark was a clever one, intended to lighten my mood. But my beloved continued. "It is not my intention to be witty. I fear the worst. Division is always a diminishment."

"So serious," I said. I returned to the bed and touched my beloved under the chin. "Too serious." The afternoon air came in slowly through an open window. We lay there, mirror images of one another. "I think that comes from being too young. You are still almost a child. With time, the seriousness will disappear."

My beloved rolled away from me. "My seriousness will disappear? And what will replace it? Do you mean to tell me that you do not take what you do seriously? That Brunetto does not? That Durante does not?"

"I cannot tell you how Durante feels," I said. Now my tone was grave, too.

∽

Seed of love, a large, triangular scrap, opens a door onto a small room, and a jug of wine, and a conversation that came pouring out of the bottle's neck. This was some months before I gave Brunetto Latini the poem I had written about my wife, and some months after I had started visiting my beloved. Durante had been cheerful when I ran into him on the street that morning. "I am working on a new verse," he said, "that will give a full account of the mysteries of love."

"You cannot hope to do that," I said.

This simple observation seemed to wound him. He fell silent at once. He did not speak when spoken to. He did not turn to look at me. For more than an hour, in fact, he did not utter a sound, and he failed to acknowledge the men we passed on the street, even when he knew them well. At length, we came to his home, and he motioned for me to sit at his table, and he poured us both full glasses of wine, and only then did he take up the thread of the conversation.

"My friend Guido," he said, "I can hope to do that. I must be able to do that. If I cannot, then I am no more than a charlatan. If I have felt love, then I must be able to give a full account of love."

"Time has passed," I said. "Has that given you purchase on your love?" Durante had loved a girl who had died a few years before. He spoke of her often, remembered how she had stood before him, the play of the light across her face and hands. Sometimes, remembering her made him quite melancholy. Other times, he became ecstatic.

He paused for a moment and took the cup of wine down from his lips. "No, no," he said. "It is not that same person. I still love her, but now I love a different person as well."

"And who is that?"

"Someone who loves another, and is loved by another. Not only a different person but a different kind of person. And it has changed me: these days I feel both joyful and wretched."

"Can you tell me more?"

He cast his eyes down for a long time. He fingered the stem of his glass. Then he lifted them and met my gaze. "I cannot," he said, saying everything.

⁓

I go through the stack of scraps. There are some scraps that mean nothing to me, *Vita Nuova*, *Campaldino*. Then there is one that reads, simply *Go*. I place it on the table next to *God made a wretch when he made you* and then speak the phrase out loud. It echoes through this humble dwelling in Sarzana.

One afternoon, Brunetto Latini and I argued with one another. We always had our differences of opinion, but they were, for the most part affectionate, softened by the comedy of his cruelty and his stubborn, theatrical silences. A few days after I gave him the poem about my wife and my beloved, I came to see him for our regular appointment. Rather than send his servant to collect me, he met me at the door himself. His eyes were sharper than I had ever seen them, and for the first time in years I noticed their color, which was a shockingly vivid green.

"I cannot see you today," he said.

"I do not understand."

"I cannot meet with you."

"What is the explanation for this?"

"I cannot explain myself," he said. "Just go."

"But my poems?"

"Please," he said. "You see me here without a jug of wine, without a single cutting word upon my lips. Isn't that enough to suggest an extraordinary circumstance? Go. Go without your poems. Go without another word. Just go."

"When will we meet again?"

"I will send for you," he said.

The city was silent that afternoon. I resolved to walk until I came upon anyone I knew—or rather, I told myself, anyone I thought I knew, since Brunetto was so changed. I walked for an hour, and then another hour, but could find no one. Just before sundown, I was due to visit my beloved. As I turned into the Piazza Santa Croce, I bumped into a man coming the other way. It was Durante.

"My first friend," he said.

"And you are mine."

"It is a quiet day today," he said. "Are you out for a stroll?"

"Yes," I said. "And you?"

"I have been sitting in the middle of the piazza. I am taking a short walk to clear my head, and then I will return to the piazza. Would you like to sit with me?"

"I cannot," I said. "I am visiting another friend. But perhaps I will see you later."

"I will be sitting right there," he said.

~

My beloved did not want to move. "You need not," I said. "You have moved enough for one day."

"As have you," my beloved said. "How is your foot?" This time, I had successfully avoided the box while getting into bed, but passion had pushed it from my mind. When I got up to walk across the room, I set down my foot and tumbled to the floor. For a few minutes, my ankle could not take my weight, but my beloved's attentions distracted me from my pain. We remained in bed, once again mirroring one another, looking out the window at the slate gray sky. Down on the plaza, Durante was exactly where he said he would be, sitting on the stone bench as still as if he, too, were stone. He liked to say that stillness was, for him, a form of movement. I did not take this as another bit of nonsense. I had seen him remain motionless for an hour while those around him drank and laughed, only to stand finally and announce to the other men that he had completed a work of verse. It was said that he could hold the outside world away from the contents of his mind. "He has a gift," Brunetto Latini liked to say to me when I mentioned Durante, "and you are a sad and simple dunce."

I had brought a copy of my new poem for my beloved, who read it intently. "Has your wife seen this?" my beloved asked.

"No," I said.

"Will she?"

"Not that copy. It is for you to keep."

"Another copy?"

"I am not certain," I said.

We returned to the bed. The clouds dissolved. The newly brilliant afternoon came pouring through the window. "Let me close the shades," I said.

"No, no," my beloved said, raising a hand to softly stay me. "Wouldn't you rather that I have a little sun than no air at all?" This was the question that hung in my mind as I sat at my beloved's writing-desk and composed a letter to my wife. Even before my beloved had made the suggestion, I had planned to write a letter; I did not know what advice Brunetto Latini would give me regarding the poem, or when his strange behavior would lift, and I believed that I owed my wife an explanation. "Wouldn't you rather that I have a little sun," I wrote to my wife, "than no air at all?" I had once believed that my wife and my beloved combined to form one ideal mate. But now I saw that one was holding me down, and that the other was offering the possibility that I might rise. I finished the letter, folded it, and placed it at the edge of the desk. When I went to look at the window again, Durante was still there. "Stop looking out the window," my beloved said. "This bed is too large for one."

When I woke again, the sun was low in the sky. I went down onto the Piazza Santa Croce, taking the stairs tenderly on account of my ankle. Durante was gone. I had come across the city slowly, but now I quickened my pace, anxious to return home. As I approached the Piazza Salvemini, I saw the figure of a man that I thought at first might be Durante. It was not: the man was older, and he was accompanied by a young boy and a horse. The man tied the horse up to the poplar, caressed its nose, and gave the boy instructions. "Sugar in the mouth," he said, "as you touch the flank. By this method, the animal will learn to trust you." The man opened a sack, let the boy scoop out sugar with cupped hands, and then departed, the sack slung over his shoulder. The boy poured the sugar from his left hand to his right hand, then switched the position of his hands and let the sugar fall back from the right to the left. It was innocent, a child's game, the rope of sugar suspended between his hands, but then a gust rushed across the plaza and scattered sugar everywhere. The boy held out his hand, offering the last bits of sugar. Instead, the horse bared his teeth and bit; a rose of blood bloomed in the boy's palm. I stepped toward the boy, but a figure had already appeared to pull him to safety. I could not tell whether this figure was a man or a woman, no matter how closely I looked, but it was old, as old as my beloved was young, with knobbed hands and white hair and watery eyes that it fixed upon me accusatorially as it gathered up the boy. The child was rescued, the horse gentled, the man summoned. When I left the piazza, I noticed that the boy was dipping his hands into the sack of sugar again.

∾

I meant to tell my wife the story, then to eat supper with her, and then to give her the letter. Though we would discuss matters in the morning, I could not speak before she read my explanation. But when I felt in my coat pocket after supper, the letter was gone. I awoke early the next morning and walked quickly to the Piazza Salvemini, where I searched for the letter. Finding nothing, I moved on to the Piazza Santa Croce. I looked in every corner, in every place where a sheet of paper might have been taken by the wind. Once I glanced up at my beloved's window. The shades were drawn. I do not remember whether I went upstairs and knocked on my beloved's door. I do not remember whether I went upstairs to see my beloved. I do not remember if I undressed or was undressed. Any of these things is possible.

I do remember, though, that in the street, as I made my way home, I encountered Brunetto Latini's servant. He was short of breath. "Guido Cavalcanti," he said, "Brunetto would like to meet with you now."

"Has he recovered from his spell of yesterday?" I said.

"Come with me," he said. He led me past the Piazza Santa Maria Novella, and into a narrow side street. Brunetto Latini was sitting on the ground, a mendicant's robe around his shoulders and a huge jug of wine at his side.

"I see that you have found your friend," I said. "And now I have found mine. I am glad of these reunions."

"Shut up, dunce," he said. "Sit. I have read the poem you left with me, the poem about your beloved."

"About my wife?"

"I think that I understand it completely. Do you want my counsel?"

"I do," I said.

"Do not be the fool you are," he said. "Your wife should not see this poem."

"Do you suggest a letter instead?"

"I suggest neither," he said. "She does not need to know a thing. Remember, a wide mouth is a grave of sorts." He took a drink from the jug and wiped his mouth on the fringe of his robe. "Have you shown the poem to anyone else?"

"Only my beloved," I said.

"Idiot," he said. "One word can start a war. I counsel silence, only silence. Say nothing. Write nothing."

"Nothing about this?"

"Nothing at all. In fact, I have helped you toward your goal." He reached into a pocket and produced my poem, which he had ripped into pieces.

"Write nothing," I say now, and replace the scrap of paper atop the pile, and move my tired body from the table to the bed.

~

I could not help but heed Brunetto Latini's advice; it was given with authority, and he had no reason to mislead me. As a result, I continued to divide my time between the Piazza Santa Croce and my home. If my wife suspected anything, she did not make her suspicions known. There were years when we were happier with each other, and years when we were less happy, and then there were years when our happiness ceased to be the issue. Around us, the city showed its teeth. Cousin took up arm against cousin. Venerable heads of families called for violence against the heads of other families. Vandals cut scars into the skins of all three trees in the Piazza Salvemini. Durante rose through the city to the rank of Prior, and Brunetto Latini died and was placed inside the earth.

I cannot remember the exact reasons that Florence split in two: papacy, heresy, fear of the mob. I know only that the thought of the city's dissolution darkened my days. "What will happen?" my beloved asked. "This will pass," I said. "The city is a living thing, and it will repair itself." I did not believe a word I said.

In those days, I saw very little of Durante. When I line up the years, there are some from which he is conspicuously absent. He was already a Prior, of course, and I was also active in the city government, and these responsibilities kept us apart.

One afternoon in summer, an unseasonable mist hung over the streets, engirdling the buildings and brushing its cold fingers against my face. It was not a day that recommended itself to walking, but I was restless, and I made my way around the entire city, resolved to go from piazza to piazza. That day I ran into Durante repeatedly. The first time, we were near the Piazza dei Ciompi; I raised my hand in greeting, but he did not acknowledge me. Then I saw him on the corner of the Piazza Santissima Annunziata, gazing up at the sky. "Durante," I called, but he did not turn. Finally, I was coming across the Piazza Santa Maria Novella when I saw him disappearing out the far end of the square. "My friend," I said. "Please, wait."

He turned toward me. The expression on his face was not one I was accustomed to seeing. His mouth was drawn into a tight line, and his eyes were aflame. "Do not call me friend," he said.

"Is something the matter?"

The concern in my voice stayed him, softened him slightly.

"Yes," he said. "But it is not something I can discuss."

"And why not?"

"There is a problem you cannot solve. More than that: it is a problem you can only make worse."

"Are you certain?"

"I do not want to discuss it," he said. He turned from me suddenly and moved down the street. He was favoring his right leg, and as he disappeared into the mist, he looked like a much older man. That day my beloved opened the door before I even reached the top of the stairs. We embraced in the doorway, and then went directly to the bed. Few words passed between us; in fact, I cannot remember any. This was not unusual. We were familiar with each other, and sometimes language had no place in our afternoons. On the way out, I kicked the box at the foot of the bed rather theatrically. "My enemy," I said. My beloved smiled, but with a distant expression.

The mist lifted on my way home. The air turned warm. The day began to smell like summer again. But the lightness in my heart did not last. My wife was at the table, her eyes red from crying. A pair of men, she said, had come to call. They were messengers from Durante, she said, and they bore three letters. The first letter was for me, and it contained orders of banishment; I was to leave Florence the following morning, and the pair of men would return to ensure that I did so. Reasons were not given. Reasons did not need to be given. As Brunetto Latini once said, "Politics is its own reason, and its own unreason." The second letter was for my wife, and it was the letter I had written years earlier, the confession I had penned in the bedroom of my beloved. My hand was that of a younger man: the script bolder, surer, deluded. The third letter, also for my wife, informed her that the relationship between me and my beloved had continued unabated for the intervening years. I took the second letter in my hand. It was warm to the touch. When I gave it back to my wife, she asked if I wanted to read the others. "No," I said. "Just tell me if Durante calls me friend." She nodded.

The last night in Florence, I lay thinking of my wife, and wishing that I could think of my beloved instead. I tried to summon a face, the feel of skin beneath my skin. I failed at it all. The men came to my door the next morning, three of them, to lead me away. One of the men had the face of a child, and the trusting manner of one as well. "Please," he said.

Please: I set this scrap down at the end of the line.

~

The first night in Sarzana, I could not sleep. This is, perhaps, predictable. But I expected that I would think of my wife or my beloved, of Durante or Brunetto Latini. I thought of none of them. Instead, my mind drifted to the incident with the horse and the boy in the Piazza Salvemini. I wish it had not. The next morning I could not remove the image from my mind, and in the months since I have come to Sarzana, I have been able to think of little else. Worse, I have not been able to prevent the memory from assuming new and fearful forms in which the injury done to the child is far worse: sometimes a hoof takes the child in the eye, sometimes it cracks the skull in half. I wake in the night, shaking so hard my bed-board chatters. I have been bringing up whatever small meals I manage to force down.

Brunetto Latini remained on the earth until he was almost eighty-five years old. I have no illusions that I will do the same. Nor will I write anything as accomplished as the *Tesoretto*. Instead, I have written a handful of new poems, as well as long letters to Durante and to my wife. I have not written to my beloved. What would I say? I am here, and not there, and it would seem redundant to describe those circumstances. I am certain that my beloved has learned of my departure from Florence. Perhaps Durante has delivered the message himself.

I have also begun a third letter to Brunetto Latini, a letter that begins by conceding the strangeness of writing to a dead man. At first, the letters were short, no more than a page each, but they have grown and grown here in Sarzana. When I can write no more, I lay my head down on the desk, which is cool and smooth, like a large, flat stone. My breath passes over the letters, over the poems, over the stack of papers. Sometimes it lifts a corner, gently pushing a scrap toward the wall. Sometimes it falls in the spaces between the things that I have written.

It is difficult to concentrate, and not only because I am forgetful. The threat of interruption is everpresent. A rap may sound at the door. It may be a local boy playing a prank. It may be the wind, angry that it cannot get at the papers inside, making do with a low-hanging tree branch. It may be a trick of memory. Or it may be a messenger bearing the news that I am welcome once again in the city where I was born. I will take hold of the mantel, steadying myself, and then nod calmly. I will allow him to depart. Then I will collect the scraps of paper to which I have committed my memories, move them to one side of the desk, take up the letters, fill a chalice to its brim with wine, and drink from it, careful not to stain the pages.

VI. Mr. Mxyztplk's Opus

Editor's Note:
This story, after several readings, still resists my interpretation. I know that there must be clues in the central character's name, but I cannot for the life of me extract them. I have sounded the word out, forward and backward, to no avail: it is possible that it exists at a level of verbal felicity either beyond me or, more likely, beneath me. One thing is certain: this Mxyztplk is a monster of some sort: a demon, a dybbuk, a dastard. In fact, I suspect that the first throb of this story originates in a story I once told Mr. Greenman. A few years back, I was staying in the Hilton Metropole on Edgeware Road, nursing a brace of disappointments, one personal and the other professional. I cannot say too much about either of them, but the combined force of their humiliation had encouraged me to leave America, albeit briefly; consequently, London. I was sitting downstairs in the hotel bar, grading student papers, not a single one of which cheered my heart (I remember one title: "Bad Heir Days: The Cosmetic Dimension of Inheritance in Victorian Fiction"), and I overheard a conversation between two men, one roughly my age, the other roughly Mr. Greenman's. Apparently, they had been close coevals, and the younger man was attempting to change the terms of the friendship. The older man resisted. At one point, he sighed voluminously and said, "It's times like this that I can't even pronounce my own name." I thought this an interesting mixture of drunken self-pity, psychoanalysis, and bon mot, and I related it to Mr. Greenman on a postcard. Now, Mr. Greenman has said in print—specifically, in the anthology *Politically Inspired: Fiction For Our Time* (MacAdam/Cage, 2003)—that this story has something to do with a character named Superman, some sort of being from outer space, and his complicity in both the propping up and undoing of

America. I can only say that his explanation smacks of folderol, and in my defense I offer up what the older man said after he said that he could not pronounce his own name: "Isn't it funny that six drinks can sometimes do what five cannot?"

This story begins, like so many have lately, in a bar. I'm writing you this letter on a placemat, the edges of which are scalloped for the sake of elegance. Even once I'm sobered up, even when I emerge from the drab light of the bar into the equally drab light of the early morning, there's no guarantee I'll be able to read most of what I've written, thanks to my penchant for tiny print and the fact that most of the text has been covered with a kudzu of doodles. Right now, I'm finishing up a complex doodle that includes a flower, an airplane, and a puckish self-portrait that's loosely based on a Claeissens. There's the imp from the Fifth Dimension who bedeviled Superman. There's the man who cannot stand.

This morning I woke up tangled in a mess of sheets with my shoes still on. Worse: I was wearing my hat, or at least had worn it into bed. It was a few inches from my head, turned on its crown like a tipped-over turtle. Whenever I have seen a turtle in that position, I have thought of it as praying, belly open to the heavens, flippers extended in helplessness and urgency. Once I used turtles as the inspiration for a bit of mischief—I took the world's fastest men and made them the world's slowest men, after which I entered them in footraces against various turtles. At the same time, I changed the laws here in the city so that the mayoral race was not determined by popular vote, but rather by foot speed. The courts tried to throw out the results; the newly elected turtle mayor was so angry that he called a press conference and spent the entire time snapping at the microphones set up in front of him. The whole mess delighted me, but then Superman, with the help of a strategically placed billboard, tricked me into saying my name backwards and I was returned to the Fifth Dimension. All the mischief I had perpetrated disappeared. Does that seem fair? I speak my own name in reverse and all my work reverses itself as well? It is said that the power to create is also the power to destroy, but I would prefer a less literal demonstration of the principle.

The barmaid just came by to ask me if I'd like another. I tapped two fingers on the lip of the glass I just drained to signal yes. Now I'm doodling a bunch of balloons. You loved balloons. You said "Anything that crashes back to earth gently is a godsend." Remember? And what of things that crash to earth ungently? What of a tower? What of a man?

Remember this? Nice fall day, little while back, we woke up calm, turned toward each other in bed, started the day right. Over my shoulder, you spotted the clock. "Shit," you said. "I have to get to work." You were hanging a show of some new artist who you told me was a "second-rate Wolfgang Lettl."

"Who's that?" I said. You were washing your face a second time, because you were still groggy. Your hair was pulled back. You looked beautiful. I was propped up in bed, pretending to read the newspaper, instead watching you in the mirror.

"Lettl? He's a second-rate Magritte."

"So does that make this painter third-rate or fourth-rate? I've lost track."

"You know," you said, breezing over to give me a kiss, "I left my slide rule at the gallery. I'll run some calculations when I get there and call you back."

That's the whole memory. It may strike you as trivial, and I suppose you're right. There's no grand narrative arc in a scene of lovers waking up, trading a bit of banter, parting for the day. The significance doesn't reside in that story, but rather the fact that, less than a year later, that story and all stories like it swiftly exited existence. Ten months later, you didn't say you'd call me. You couldn't.

I blame myself. This is what I tell them all. I blame myself. You should have seen me, I tell them. "Can you describe yourself before the incident?" they say. One of them even gave me a pad of paper and a pencil and asked me to draw myself. I got as far as the purple bowler, the wide collar, the upturned nose, and then

I turned the pencil into a dandelion and blew the head away with one emphatic outbreath.

This story may amuse you (you liked anything that involved flowers), but it sweetens a bitter truth: these days, I can only describe myself to myself, and that's too much to bear. My drink has arrived, gin and tonic, a double. Waitresses love me, especially since I'm going through a "keep the change" phase.

Where was I? Oh, yes: describing myself to myself. For starters, try to fathom a lifetime of mischief. I'm sure I asked you this when we started dating. Now I'm asking again. Try to imagine thirty years of plaguing Superman with the kind of practical jokes that would have been a scream back in the Fifth Dimension but which in Metropolis only got me collared. "Criminal mischief," the judge said after the first arrest, and put me in jail for the weekend. I levitated to eight feet in the middle of the cell and—poof!—vanished in a plume of smoke. Loose again, I made grass grow out of the tops of people's heads, turned fire hydrants into soda fountains, gave dogs the power to speak, until Superman came along and sent me packing. In those days, the abruptness of the expulsion from earth, the way in which my return to the Fifth Dimension undid all the mischief I had so carefully choreographed, drove me to distraction. I determined to return as soon as I could, and within a few months, I was back, dimming people's sunglasses until they turned black, letting apple trees come to life and hurl their fruit at passersby, causing every phone number dialed to miss its target by a single digit.

For almost three decades, I tipped and twirled the world, turned it on its ear. Then one day Superman put me back in the Fifth Dimension and I didn't feel a thing. No rage. No desire for revenge. Nothing. That's when I decided to retire. The decision wasn't as abrupt as it may seem; in my recent visits to the earth, I had spent less time devising new forms of mischief, and more time visiting museums. I have always loved human art; we don't have much of it at all where I come from, as every man fancies himself an artist and, as a result, no man earns the right to the distinction. While one might assume from my own work that my tastes would tend toward pop art and surrealism, I actually prefer the Flemish landscapes of the late sixteenth century. The scope impresses me, as well as the water, the rivers that wind through the mountainous landscapes. I'm not an art historian, so I can't do much more than tell you that I love those rivers, that although they don't really resemble living rivers, they produce the same emotions in me, a feeling at once infinitesimal and infinite, both of being dwarfed by and of participating in the sublime. And then there are the habitations clustered in the middle distance, the little villages hanging halfway up a mountain, just waiting to be disarranged. I have thought of some of my best ideas while staring into the frame of a Coninxloo or a Bol.

At any rate, I had read that a small museum downtown was hanging its collection of van Orley, who has always struck me as a bit too early, though what I probably mean by that is a bit too decorative. Still, Flemish is Flemish. When I got to the museum there were as many people as paintings: five. Two women huddled around a portrait of Charles V. Two men sentinelled a study for the Job altarpiece. "Such turbulence," one man said.

"And there are wings, too," I said. "Maybe van Orley invented the airplane."

The second man laughed, though I saw then that it wasn't a man. It was a woman, a thin tall woman with a severe haircut and a black suitcoat. It was you. We stood there for a while. You introduced yourself, then introduced me to Paul. "Would the two of you like to get lunch?" I said.

"I think Paul has somewhere to be, but I'll grab a bite," you said.

At lunch, you proved better than me at almost everything. Better at putting a new acquaintance at ease. Better at laughing brightly at jokes that weren't necessarily funny. Better at relating the particulars of your life up until then—though, to be fair, you were not yet thirty, and so your life had spanned only a tiny fraction of mine. I asked after your husband or boyfriend. "Oh, no," you said, "I'm just a single egg frying in a pan."

"Are you saying you want breakfast?" I said. You laughed and looked right at me, and it shamed me. I had seen it all, or at least most of it. But the thought of a beautiful young woman looking into my eyes and finding herself not only reflected there, but also somehow completed—that left me dumb. A month later, we moved in together, into an apartment building with halls so narrow they gave the couch trouble.

When you asked me what I had done with myself all the years before I met you, I answered the only way I knew how: honestly. I told you that I had been in the business of creating mischief. Later I saw that you must have taken me for some kind of intelligence operative, or maybe even a common criminal, but you didn't ask any other questions, and that furnished yet more proof of your perfection. As for that mischief, I renounced it entirely, and we went on, newly paired, suddenly possible. We made friends, we took trips, we stayed too long in restaurants; the young art dealer, the old mischief-maker.

Mischief, mischief, mischief. The word has started to break apart on me. Mis chief. I doodle an Indian maiden. That's her: Miss Chief. She has a feather that squirts water at you when you try to smell it. I must have said *water* out loud. The waitress just brought me a glass. But water calls for sterner stuff. Time to deaccession another Alexander Hamilton from my collection. Do you know about gin? Soon after its introduction into Britain in the early eighteenth century, it flowed like water through the lower classes. The rich both demonized it as the source of the nation's moral rot and depended upon it financially as a result of taxes. Consumption peaked in the early 1740s, when an average Londoner drank more than two gallons per person per year. This strikes me as amateurish. The gin that minutes ago filled the glass in front of me is gone.

Gone. It's not a word I understand very well. For me, gone has always referred to a temporary condition, to something that is about to come back. When Superman banished me, I only had to wait a few months to return, until the border between the earth and the Fifth Dimension relaxed, so no matter how angry I felt, my departure always had a comic air about it. That's why I laughed when I first came home that day. Unlike so much else in my life, I remember it perfectly: I shook a light morning rain from the umbrella, removed my boots in the hall, and entered to find a note on the table. "Can't do it any longer. Can't explain, can't apologize, can't discuss. Please don't call me." I chuckled. "Poof!" I said. But the hours passed, and then day gave way to night. By midnight the comedy had drained away.

When you left I went down to the corner and then around the bend. The only response to a mad world is madness. Was that Celine? That was also when I returned to painting. I had begun just a few months before I met you, anticipating my retirement, and while the canvases had only failure on them from the start, every once in a while a corner would come to life. I recall one in particular, a pastiche of the Garden of Delights. Most of it was boilerplate, but one section stood out as if illuminated. In it, a rabbit with wings drove a train toward a tunnel whose edge bore a Latin inscription. I can't retrieve the translation precisely, but it followed these rough contours: "Here he lies without a multitude of brethren." Near him, a bird with human arms held a mirror that reflected the inscription. I was trying, in my own clumsy way, to explain my relationship to the earthly world. For years, each time I visited here I came through a kind of tunnel. Each time, I could only return to those like me (the rabbit with wings is no doubt a close cousin of the bird with human arms) by speaking my name backwards, in mirror image (it is what the linguists in our land call *logos reversus*, though a simple translation cannot communicate the rich cultural history behind the phrase). When I think on the painting now, I see another dimension to its meaning, one I could not have understood at the time: I passed through a lifetime of darkness to find a mate, and then I lost her.

By now my cramped block print has completely covered the placemat. I doodle a computer over the word *compute* and a movie screen over the word *movie*. Then I doodle the fatal crescent shape of California. California, California. Damn California to hell. Weeks after you left the apartment I discovered through a mutual friend that you had booked a trip to Los Angeles, perhaps to buy art, perhaps to visit relatives. I will never know for certain, but I do know that my heart turned instantly to black ice. I assumed that the motive was a man, that the trip would include weeks in another lover's arms. So I came out of retirement for one final act of mischief.

I should sober up enough to explain myself clearly, or at the very least, let six drinks do what five cannot. I put the idea in his head. I saw his eyes shift from sandstone to quartz, from dull and mean to brilliantly cruel. I saw the plan bloom inside him. This isn't to say he was innocent before. The seed requires fertile soil, and the sour ocean of a sick mind refuses no river. I struggle for a beautiful metaphor in the hopes that I can earn pity through grace. I fail. What I mean to say is that I ordered only a hijacking. Take the plane, I urged him, in silence, in mischief. Take it somewhere else. I knew you would be aboard. I wanted you to feel pure fear, and for that fear to ripen into a desire for me. Instead, I set it all in motion; my dead heart threw off a final spark and caused a conflagration. This isn't by way of apology. I am beyond apology. For days, for weeks, I have come to bars, sometimes this one, sometimes the one down the street, and thought this through, suffered not only for what I have done but for what I have been unable to do. It would take a single word, a single familiar word, to erase the hell this world has become and redraw what the world was: not perfect but without that one atrocity, all things in their rightful places. All things but one, that is. If I unmake what I have made, you will still be on that plane, will still be heading west, will still be moving away from me. Once, years ago, after a particularly satisfying episode of mischief involving a swordfish and a typewriter, Superman landed in front of me and asked a question that was more devastating than any violent blow he could have delivered. "What do you want?" he said. What, indeed? I only knew what I did not want. Now I could answer his question, definitively, with the confidence of a dead man, could stand, take off my hat, and say without a doubt that I want you, that I want a world where I can hold you once again, feel the full length of your body alongside mine, where I can push the hair away from your ear and tell you that we should see a movie, go to dinner, go to bed, that we should travel, that I love you so much that I cannot any longer keep my hold on my own existence, that I slip down the incline, away from my desires, toward the broad lake at the bottom of the hill, the lake that means annihilation by a single word, by the word that will, when I finally capitulate to my duty and my sorrow, escape my mouth like a bird from a cage, like a soul from a dying body, like a seed from the head of a dandelion:

KLTPZYXM!

V. A Big Fight Scene Between Two Men with the Same Name

Editor's Note:

Though this short piece masquerades as a bit of slapstick, it is in fact among the most telling moments in the entire book. As we know by now, true artwork is created by two men, a mentor and a protégé. The protégé does most of the work and often receives most of the credit, but the mentor is no less vital to the process. Here, Mr. Greenman imagines work done by two men, but rather than represent it as the natural division between mentor and protégé, he concocts a senselessly disturbing scenario: he says that it is a fight between two men with the same name, but it is evident that it is a fight inside one man, one creator, and that there is not a mentor in sight. The result? Despair, plain and simple, at least as it is defined by Kierkegaard: *fortvivelse*, which refers not to a division of the self but to a doubling.

Ray hit Ray on the shoulder first, and then Ray hit Ray on the nose. This sent Ray reeling, but as he fell backwards he managed to rake his right arm across Ray's face, opening up a cut to the immediate left of Ray's nose. Ray still had the upper hand, though, and shoved Ray hard with both hands, finalizing Ray's fall to the ground. For a few seconds, Ray stood over Ray in triumph. When Ray bent down to exult over Ray's fallen body, though, Ray grabbed his hair, which Ray wore long, and tugged it as hard as he could. Ray collapsed next to Ray on the floor, and Ray jumped up quickly and began kicking Ray. Ray wore boots, and he used the hard point and the heel expertly, both getting at Ray's ribs and working the tender areas around the kidneys. Ray found a metal ruler on the ground, and managed to whack Ray across the shins, and then to bury the corner of the ruler in Ray's knees. At that, Ray collapsed in pain, and, clutching his knee, lost his balance. His downward progress had serious consequences for Ray; Ray's knees were propelled into Ray's throat, and Ray groaned and rolled over onto his side. Ray crawled toward the door, convinced that the blunt force of his knees upon Ray's neck had finished Ray off, but as he stretched his hand toward the knob, he felt an explosion at the base of his neck. It was Ray. He was brandishing a pool cue—where on earth had that come from, Ray wondered? Ray struck Ray with the cue twice against the back of the head, and then held it like a battering ram, with the tapered end toward Ray. Ray drew himself to his feet and rushed at Ray with all his strength. The maneuver had the desired effect, driving the tip of the cue into Ray—in fact, into his left hip, where it ripped Ray's shirt and tore into Ray's skin. Ray stood; though his legs were wobbly, he felt his strength returning. He faced off against Ray, who had also pulled himself to his feet, and the two of them began raining blows on one another. Ray's fist went into Ray's eye. Ray's fist went into Ray's ear. Ray gouged at Ray's eyes. Ray got Ray in a headlock and thumped his nose with the flat of his palm. Ray's hands were slick with Ray's blood, and Ray wondered how much longer Ray could go on like this.

IV. STRUGGLE IN NINE

Editor's Note:
   Those who still doubt the structural sophistication of this novel should doff their caps to this section; while the book comprises two nine-part movements and a dense center, there is, inset in the second half, like a gem, a story with nine parts. Our experience with "Notes from a Paper" teaches us to look at the middle part, section five. This has exactly one hundred words, a perfectly round number that , maddeningly, has no center—and which points proleptically to the last story in this collection.

I.

Cautious, he picked up the magazine. Interested, he read it from cover to cover. Amused, he laughed. Transfixed, he gasped. Gratified, he wrote a letter to the editor commending the magazine. Eager, he picked up the next month's issue. Surprised, he found that his letter was printed in the "Letters to the Editor" column. Emboldened, he wrote another one. Amazed, he saw that his second letter was printed as well. He took a long look in the mirror. The mirror had a flaw on the right hand side that always looked like a scar on his skin. He traced the scar with his right hand. Altered, he was. Altered, and changed. What he had been before, he no longer remained.

II.

The eagle of communism swooped down and grabbed the rabbit of capitalism. The general woke up sweating. He grabbed his gun and ran into the garden. Was there an Arab? Was there a killer? Was there a point to be made? The general sat down on a bench and hung his head. In movies he had seen, generals were always brave. They were often corrupt, but they were always brave. Their faces turned red when they were accused of cowardice. They pounded their fists on tables and stood ramrod-straight when they inspected the troops. The general felt an ant skirt the flannel edge of his pajamas and he began to shriek, for ants had killed his son and now they were coming for him.

III.
Girl in bar: Are you a good writer?
Me: Yeah. I mean, I think so. I have good ideas and attach good words to them.
Girl in bar: I am a good dancer.
Me: Really?
Girl in bar: No. Not really. But when girls say they are dancers, boys tend to like it.
Me: That's funny. That's why I said I was a writer.
Girl in bar: You're not?
Me: No, I am. But that's why I said it. Sometimes there are happy coincidences.

IV.
I have a friend. She writes miniatures. I love them. I love her. Her pieces are short. Ten words at most. But they sing. This piece, the piece I am writing, is already too long. Even section IV is too long. "You are bloated and incontinent," she said. "You don't know how to control yourself. A story is about a flower that bends slightly under the breath of a dog. No more than that. 'A flower bends slightly under the breath of a dog.' Man, that's long. I want to cut out some words. I will cut out 'slightly.' Now it has nine words. Now I am happier with it. Will you take me to dinner to celebrate?" We go to dinner. We drink too much wine. We end up at her place, on her couch. She takes my head in her hands. My lips rise to meet hers.

V.

Birds don't write. They are God's creatures, of course, God's chosen creatures, in some sense, for they fly more closely to His Divine Providence than any of us can hope to, but despite their privileged station they cannot write. When they see a rabbit, they can only choose whether or not to kill it. Is this a form of writing? It is certainly a plot. It most certainly reveals character. Time, someone once told me, is what keeps everything from happening all at once. History, I retorted, is what ensures that everything has happened. We each thought ourselves the cleverer.

VI.

I have a friend. She writes miniatures. She tells me that my pieces have too much plot. I cannot understand what she means. To my eye, they have no plot. "You are always sending and receiving like a radio station or a radio," she says. "You are always doing what should never be done. I am going to put on my pants and leave." She leaves. I turn on the radio. There is a song on the radio about a girl who leaves. I turn off the radio. There is a bird flying outside. It banks in the air and heads right toward my window. I close my eyes, afraid of what I will see.

VII.

Me: Yes, I do love you. But not the way you need me to. I think that sometimes you're too afraid.
Girl in bar: I was afraid of that.
Me: Not everything is a joke. That's why I wish you wouldn't talk.
Girl in bar: Yes. I know. But when a girl decides not to talk, she disappears. And I'm afraid of disappearing.
Me: Really?
Girl in bar: That's why I never finish anything I start, so that there's a reason still to be here.
Me: No. I mean, I don't understand. You leave things undone so that you will not vanish? You're in a bad way.
Girl in bar: Are you in a good way?

VIII.

The third of March fell on the second of March. It wasn't a very common occurrence, and as such it was noteworthy. The man on the telephone was eager to make a sale, and so he divulged the secrets of the calendar. Would the lady be interested in learning how one day became the next? Did she possess an understanding of midnight? The man on the telephone hung up and took a deep breath. Most of the women he called demonstrated no interest in the calendar. They asked him if he knew of a place they could buy shoes, or books. Occasionally they had a thing for carpets. The man felt the telephone looking at him and felt afraid. He pounded a fist on the table and felt even more afraid. He picked up a magazine and began to read.

IX.

When he began to read, he knew that he would soon begin to write. But when he began to write, he knew he would not finish. Would not, and could not. He forced his mind ahead in time. He saw the seam where the day turned into the next day, and tried to imagine that his writing was a bridge across that seam, which was widening by the second. He saw the scar where one day was ripped away from the day that had preceded it. He went for a walk. He sat down, exhausted. He continued on again, rested. He searched for a place to stop and eat, famished. He spoke to an old man in uniform, lonely. He spoke to a pretty girl, attracted. He wandered, disoriented. He saw a bird, comforted. He thought it God, converted.

III. In Shuvalov's Library

Editor's Note:

Mr. Greenman's preoccupation with painting portraits of certain kinds of men—recluses, incessant catalogers—recalls Jung's remarks in the Tavistock lectures of 1935, in which he surmised that men sought psychology to reassure themselves that there were crazier specimens. This case is slightly different, in that Ivan Shuvalov, the protagonist, is a renowned curator and archivist who did, in fact, assemble the collection of the Empress Elizaveta Petrovna.

He knew English. That's why it was troubling, the "I" that he inked inside the front cover of every volume, before every occurrence of his last name. But it was not troubling on its own. It was troubling for the dollop of punctuation that followed, designed as a period but slyly canted in the direction of a comma. "I, Shuvalov," he wrote, and set down his pen.

A line of seventy words joined him to the empress. "Elizaveta Petrovna," he wrote, and then wrote sixty-eight words more. Among them were the words "acquisition," "collection," and "artistry." The line of words was also a line of argument: he was reminding the empress that he needed a building in which he could display the paintings, sculptures, and rare books he had collected over the years. "I have noted many times that acquisition itself is a form of artistry," he said, "and for that alone I should need a museum."

In the years since he had come to court—more than ten years, he said whenever he was asked—Shuvalov made the same request every week; that was how things were done with the empress. He already had the record of the museum: his catalog was comprehensive, and included every book, painting, etching, sculpture, and objet d'art that he had persuaded the empress to purchase. *Collection* was the title he had given to the first book, and *Collection, Section II* to its successor. He had filled four volumes thus far, all leather-bound, and was now working on the fifth section. Just that morning he had entered a painting that showed a solitary man alone in a room, gazing out a high, small window. The room was drab and poorly lit; the world outside the window was dominated by a round, green tree, the branches of which sparkled with brightly colored birds. Shuvalov knew why he was attracted to the painting. He even looked a bit like the man in the room; he had the same deep-set eyes, the same strong chin. The man in the room was handsome, as was Shuvalov himself. But he felt as if the painting misrepresented the truth. In his mind, the world inside his study was far superior, because it contained hundreds of possibilities, whereas the world outside the window was limited to a single existence, fixed by the artist's imagination. The painting was attributed to an artist named Bassano, a lesser contemporary of Tintoretto, though one of the previous owners had endeavored to prove that it was the work of the master himself. Shuvalov was not in the business of judging these kinds of claims; he had merely noted it in the margins of his entry and moved on. Even if he had been able to determine whether or not the painting was a Tintoretto, he could not have done so from his study: like most of the works in the *Collection,* it was elsewhere in the palace. He had only notes that described it: scraps of paper, letters submitted by other members of the court, his own jottings. Taken as a set, they added up to the painting; the sum of all these words was a picture.

The method by which the *Collection* was created was painstaking. Another man might have devised a quicker procedure, but for Shuvalov the success of a process came from the amount of control it demanded of its operator. From the various documents of description, he transferred the name of each work, its medium, a brief characterization, the date it came into the possession of the empress, its previous provenance, and so forth. He assigned each work a number, and determined whether any other works were related, either by artist, by period, or by subject. "This *Collection*," he had written to the empress in one of his earlier letters, "will one day itself be recognized as an artwork—then, perhaps, it, too, can be entered into the *Collection*." One small stroke of cleverness was enough for Shuvalov. He concluded the letter and sealed it.

~

When Shuvalov had first arrived at court, he had not permitted visitors into his chambers. "It is a sanctuary," he had announced to the attentive circle of eyes and ears. His youth had attracted visitors, and not just his youth, but the way it conspired with his high position in the court to produce a collar of importance around him. "It is a sanctuary, and that it why it must be located at the end of the longest hall in the palace." He tried to affect a lonely air.

The ladies of the court had taken an immediate interest in him, both as a result of his solitary nature and as a result of his appearance; he was told by the women, even the empress herself, that he was a handsome man. One woman had a profile that was a lesson in severity but was unaccountably beautiful. Another woman had wide eyes that were always in a state of agitation. Shuvalov remembered asking her to close her eyes and then he remembered kissing the lids softly. Beneath his lips, the lids had the feel of butterflies. A third woman had a strong back upon which his fingers moved slowly, as if half-asleep. When he took his leave after an assignation, Shuvalov would go directly to his chambers; he would use the walk down the hall to recover every detail of the woman, naming his memories, filing them.

But all this was long ago, when he had first come to court. Over the years, Shuvalov had observed that the women at court seemed to desire his company less and less. He still came to court, because his presence was required, but he no longer needed to affect a lonely air. His loneliness was actual, and some days palpable.

Though Shuvalov's life at court was without women, the circle around him had not dissipated. Where women once stood, there were now men, and they touched their beards thoughtfully as Shuvalov spoke, and murmured noises of agreement or dissent. The faces of the men had changed regularly for a number of years, and then, for a number of years, they had stayed the same. There was Prince Pyotor, who had lost a foot in combat and descanted bitterly on a wide range of topics; Prince Alexsandr, a small man who smoked small cigars, which he gripped between his stained teeth; and Prince Sergei, a thin man who liked to let loose a high, pealing laugh that was as wild as his hair, which hung around his head like the mane of a lion. The three of them had asked him more about the library, over a longer period of time, than anyone else, and this familiarity had encouraged a sort of presumption. The princes had, as long as Shuvalov could remember, asked him when he might allow them to see this majestic book, the *Collection*, that contained within it a full account of all the artwork that had earned the approval of the crown. "Never," Shuvalov said. He had explained his reasoning so many times that he no longer felt it necessary to elaborate.

∼

When Shuvalov was not making entries in the ledger-books of the *Collection*, he liked to read in philosophy, usually Augustine, which filled him with a mixture of sorrow and satisfaction. Like Augustine, he believed in setting aside parts of the self to strengthen the remaining parts. That was why the Bassano bothered him; it suggested that when the man was done mastering the contents of the room, he could simply go to the window and be delivered into a new world. Shuvalov believed otherwise. A man could cast his lot either with the room or with the window, but not both. He caressed the skin of *Collection, Section V* and turned his chair so that he faced the door to his study.

Shuvalov stared at the door. For years, he had thought nothing of it; it was merely a mahogany panel interposed between him and the long hall, the longest in the palace, the hall where he made peace daily with his solitude. Recently, though, as he came down the long hall, he began to feel as though he was being followed. At first, it was just a vague suspicion, but then, one day, he had heard the sound of footfalls behind him, moving at the same rate that he moved. When he turned around, though, he saw no one, and it did not seem to matter how fast he turned around—he could not catch so much as a glimpse of a figure darting into one of the small side rooms that lined the hall. When he resumed walking, the sound behind him also resumed, and it took a great deal of concentration, applied over a number of days, before he could be certain that it was not simply the sound of his own footsteps, trailing behind him by some accident of acoustics. That same analysis seemed to rule out certain suspects: it was unlikely to be Pyotor, for his peg would not only have given his gait a different sound but would have prevented him from moving quickly; similarly, Shuvalov was fairly certain that he would have noticed Sergei's wild hair, or that something about the situation would have induced the prince to let go with one of his wild blasts of laughter.

His inability to solve the mystery of the footsteps did not bother him, for the footsteps were not the problem. Or rather, they were not the extent of the problem. For they were only the cocking of the trigger; the firing of the weapon was the knocking that came on the door of his chambers every afternoon, a sharp report that sounded so loudly that he thought it might be his own bones banging together. The first time it happened, he had flinched violently and accidentally dragged his pen across a catalog entry for a Bruyn landscape, disfiguring it. Works had been dispatched from the Empress's holdings before through sale, or extracted through theft, and their catalog records had been deleted accordingly, but this was the first time that Shuvalov could remember nullifying one of the entries in the *Collection* as a result of his own error. He sat at his desk, his heart pounding, waiting for a second knock, but none came.

Until, that is, the next day, which brought another single knock, another blow to his heart: he had stood quickly and pulled the door open, but no one was there. The third day, too, he had opened the door after the knock to find an empty hallway. Then he began to notice that the knock was coming at the same time each day, at exactly two o'clock. The fifth day, he set aside the *Collection* at ten minutes to two and crouched by the door, ready to fling it open. The knock came at two; he opened the door; he found nothing. And each morning, as he came down the long hall to his chambers, the footsteps were still there, evasive, impossible to certify, like a face in a dream.

Though the footsteps irritated him and the knocking terrified him, Shuvalov discussed neither phenomenon at court. If the culprit was present there, his disclosure would only be a source of malicious pleasure. Whether or not the knocking was a subject of conversation, it was quickly becoming apparent to Shuvalov that it was disrupting his daily routine. He found that he could not concentrate in the late morning and early afternoon, because his anticipation was so powerful. Some days he tried to brace himself for the noise. Other days he tried to ignore it. Nothing he did seemed to have any effect. Soon, Shuvalov began to lose sleep at night, and that took an even greater toll during the day— he was in a stage of nervous agitation while he was walking through the palace taking down the particulars of paintings or sculptures that had been acquired but not yet fully recorded. Worse, he began to make errors in his entries: spelling errors, errors in date of acquisition. He became so embarrassed by the condition of *Section V* that he decided to copy its contents into an entirely new ledger, a decision that set him back almost two weeks. "Elizaveta Petrovna," he wrote in one of his weekly letters, "I have begun to consider the possibility that there may be a better method for recording the contents of your collection." He did not send the letter to the empress, but he could not forget how close he had been to sending it, and the thought brought him shame. Shuvalov had seen a man bleed for hours from a pinprick; just so, the one small fissure that had opened up in his day threatened to swallow his collection, which had become, through a steady setting aside of all other tasks, his life's work.

~

When Shuvalov could not concentrate on the *Collection*, he blamed the knocking. But there were also times when he admitted to himself that there was another distraction working on him. He had met a woman. More accurately, he had seen a woman at court, and had found that even after she passed out of his sight, she did not pass out of his mind. This woman was standing underneath an archway in one of the main ballrooms, near one of the large windows that looked out over the gardens. She did not speak to Shuvalov. From what he saw, she did not speak to anyone. Her hair was as black as ink, and her dress a cream color that reminded him of parchment. She leaned against the wall and stared into the middle distance. Shuvalov was talking to Pyotor and Sergei when he first noticed the woman. He could have asked the princes if they knew her name, but he was not willing to reveal his interest. Instead, he engineered a small deceit: he wondered aloud about the architecture of the garden, and specifically about an aspect of it that he knew was foreign to both Sergei and Pyotor. "You cannot answer me?" he said, when he knew they could not. Then, feigning impatience, he walked to the window to settle the matter for himself.

On his way to the window, he turned on his heel and stared rather shamelessly at the woman. She could not have been more than twenty years old. But she had pieces of other women in her face, in the sharp angles of her nose and cheeks, in her tight, thin mouth. And her eyes were extraordinary: dark with golden flecks in them. As a younger man, Shuvalov had believed that a woman's eyes were portals to another world, but the years had divested him of this foolish notion. Now, though, he felt as though his wisdom was abandoning him.

The woman did not appear to notice Shuvalov. If she did

notice him, she gave no sign. She continued to stare into the center of the ballroom, at nothing in particular. He pretended to look out the window at the garden—though in fact he looked at his own reflection, and judged himself to be still quite handsome. After waiting what he thought was an appropriate amount of time, he returned to Pyotor and Sergei. "The answer is obvious," he said, "if you would only look for yourself."

That evening, he thought of little except the woman, and the next day, when he was not worrying about the knock on the door, he was lost in his memory of her. He wondered if he would see her that afternoon, and when he did not, he wondered about the following afternoon. "Elizaveta Petrovna," he wrote in another letter he did not send to the empress, "when a man's heart thaws, it can be a painful process, even crippling. I must confess that there are days when the *Collection* seems as if it might be better served by another hand, and by a clearer mind. Mine has become muddied of late, I am afraid." After wasting the better part of a week, he began a new week with a renewed sense of purpose: he was scheduled to log a host of new works, including a Ghezzi etching of an Italian piazza, empty save for a man, boy, and a horse, and three trees that stood behind them like sentries. But he could not concentrate on it, or remember the other works to which it bore a resemblance, and instead he got up and walked to the court. The woman was nowhere to be found, and he came back to his chambers almost immediately, without thinking even once about the footsteps that he was quite sure, upon reflection, were padding along behind him. And then the knock, at two o'clock, nearly killed him, so violent was the noise, and he was unable to accomplish anything for the rest of the afternoon.

∽

After laboring under the influence of these distractions for three weeks, Shuvalov was so exhausted that he could hardly stay awake in the quiet of his chambers, and that, combined with his curiosity about the young woman he had seen in the ballroom, encouraged him to spend more time than usual in the court. He liked to sit on one of the green divans that was positioned in a doorway off of one of the large sitting-rooms, and to let the rest of the group arrange itself in a crescent around him. What happened in the crescent, even with an exhausted Shuvalov, was precisely what had happened before. There was Prince Pyotor haranguing another young prince about the unreadiness of the Empress's military forces. There was Prince Alexsandr, his cigar moving across the room as a rifle might. There was Prince Sergei, laughing chaotically, like something that had spilled. And yet, it was entirely different as well. Once, Shuvalov had enjoyed the company of these men, if only because their questions and remarks helped focus him on the library; now, his suspicion fell across them like a shadow. In addition, the men seemed to go rougher with him; they had always teased him about his working habits, but now Shuvalov detected a sharp edge to their comments. "It seems to be wearing on you, this use of pen and paper," Prince Sergei said one afternoon. "I can see how that would tax a man to his limit." Then he threw back his head and brayed. Shuvalov was not listening closely to Sergei; he was looking over his head at the crowd, trying to locate either the woman he had seen or the men who might be plaguing him by knocking at his door.

Shuvalov had ruled out some of the men as a result of their intelligence, their habits, or their temperaments. One of the men who Shuvalov knew to be innocent, Nikolai, was a tall young prince who spoke softly, with a deep voice that was a great source of pleasure for the women at court. He was a new arrival, and as a result still spent much of his time expressing admiration for the library, and hoping he might one day see the collection. "I cannot imagine how much discipline it must take to achieve what you have achieved," he said. "You must show it to others before you present it to the empress." Shuvalov expressed his reluctance, as he had done dozens of times before, and Nikolai grew more and more exercised, as young princes had done dozens of times before. "There is something endlessly fascinating about a record of artworks, even more fascinating than the artworks themselves," he said. "If you summarize a Hogarth print with a few brief pieces of information, such as its title, the date of its purchase, and its size, you are giving it a more honest account of its existence than a man who goes on at great length about the characters in the work, their motives and machinations. You permit another man to imagine a work of art rather than insist on one particular imagination, and that is a form of heroism."

"You speak as ardently as a student," said Shuvalov, smiling a smile he did not quite feel.

The prince laughed as if Shuvalov had been making a joke. "This is my point precisely," the prince said. "We are all students in this life. There are no teachers, only texts. We are taught by direct contact with artworks, not by the encounters between those works and other minds."

The prince went on at such length that Shuvalov's eyelids began to droop. "I must go," he said. "If not to work, then to sleep."

"Will you give me a time that I might stop by?" the Prince said.

It occurred to Shuvalov suddenly that Nikolai might be of use in helping him to identify the mystery visitor. He had been thinking of Hogarth ever since Nikolai had mentioned him, and his mind had drifted into an etching in which an older man sets a snare to catch a younger man he suspects of cuckolding him. "How about the end of next week?" Shuvalov said, low enough that no one else would hear. "At two o'clock. But if you mention the appointment to anyone, I will not honor it."

Nikolai laughed with delight. "Your secret is safe with me."

~

Shuvalov would have been perfectly happy not to have seen Nikolai until he arrived at chambers at the end of the following week. The more he reflected upon the young prince's earnest face, the more unpleasant he found it. But a few nights after his initial conversation, he encountered Nikolai again. This time he had a woman on his arm. They were coming down one of the main halls in the palace, heads bent toward each other, and Shuvalov heard soft laughter passing between them. "Ivan Ivanovich," the prince called out. Shuvalov slowed reluctantly. It was not until they had stopped that Shuvalov recognized the woman as his woman, the young woman from the ballroom. She was as beautiful as he remembered, and she carried the knowledge of that beauty in her face. "Good day," Nikolai said.

"Good day," Shuvalov said.

"Ivan Ivanovich Shuvalov. This is the Countess Natalya."

"Have we met?" Shuvalov said. He knew they had not. But he thrilled to the faint possibility that she might say yes. Perhaps they had met. Perhaps they were intimates from long ago. He had a full command of all the artwork in the empress's possession, of all the entries in the *Collection*, but he could not be counted upon to remember all that had happened in his own life, could he? Shuvalov looked into her eyes, and for her part the countess did not look away.

"No," she said.

"We are on our way to a dance," Nikolai said. "But I will see you at the end of next week." Suddenly, Shuvalov found himself angry with the prince.

"Yes," Shuvalov said. "In fact, I am happy to have seen you. I have something to discuss with you on that score."

"Ivan Ivanovich," Nikolai said, "I hope you are not reconsidering."

"No," Shuvalov said, "I just wonder if you would like to bring the countess to our appointment."

Nikolai looked at Shuvalov with surprise. "But you are so reluctant to take even a single visitor."

"I think we can make an exception for the lady," he said. He turned toward the countess and extended a hand. "I would be flattered if you would accompany the prince to my chambers on Friday at two o'clock."

That day, Shuvalov went down the long hall remembering

what he had said to the countess, and what she had said in return. And when the two o'clock report sounded, he heard it only faintly; he had sped through the Ghezzi etching, and a Guercino canvas of the martyrdom of St. Catherine, and a painting by Cranach the Elder of two lovers in repose.

～

It was now the appointed day, and the clock was nearing the appointed hour, and Shuvalov was trying to enter a few more items before the prince and the countess arrived. He had recently purchased a plan of the city of Vienna, two pieces of Roman statuary, and a book on numismatics, and he recorded them in *Collection, Section V*. His favorite of the new acquisitions was a wonderful Arcimboldo, a painting on panel in which the subject's features were represented by fruits, vegetables, and flowers. The man in the picture had a nose that was a radish and ears that were ears of corn. A flower bloomed in the center of his forehead. It was a small enough work that Shuvalov had it with him in his chambers, propped up on the edge of his desk where he could look at it while he entered it into the *Collection*. Shuvalov felt a kinship with the portrait—he sometimes felt as if he, too, was not fully embodied, but rather built up from components, in his case the works of art he recorded in the *Collection*. He imagined explaining this to the countess when she remarked on the strangeness of the Arcimboldo, which he was certain she would.

But the Arcimboldo failed where the letter to the Empress had failed before it, and before long Shuvalov was asleep. Even in his sleep, he continued to work on the *Collection*. But he found, to his dismay, that he was not entering works that he had acquired for the Empress. He looked around the library, or rather the library he was dreaming while he slept in his library, and found that the colors in the room were brilliant: greens and blues and yellows that leapt out at him. The reds were especially vivid, sometimes the hue of a sunset, sometimes the hue of fresh blood. Shuvalov marked them down, privately consoling himself with the knowledge that these colors were imaginary. Life was nowhere near that bold.

His eyes fluttered open, and then were drawn into sleep once more. He braced for the knock. When it came, it was tentative, delicate. He went to the door, and opened it, and was surprised to find Natalya standing on the other side of the door by herself. She had a strange expression on her face. "I was not prepared for the long walk down the hall," she said. Then she stepped forward, and as she came through the doorway her gown fell away from her, and she stood naked before him. He thought she was beautiful, and must have said something, because she returned the compliment. "You are more beautiful than I," she said. She spoke in English, a language Shuvalov did not know she possessed.

Shuvalov looked at Natalya, who was now so close to him that he could smell the scent of her body. She moved a hand over his hand; her flesh was warm and smooth, which made him fear suddenly that his was cold and rough. "These are your eyes," she said, brushing a finger across the skin beside his eyes. "This is your nose. This is your mouth." She repeated the same procedure in reverse on her own face, with his fingertips, guiding him as she went. "Now sit," she said. "And tell me all that you have seen."

He sat, her hand on his shoulder like a benediction, and recorded her entry into the room in *Collection, Section V*. "Natalya," he wrote. "Appeared at door wearing gown. Came through doorway. Stood naked beside desk. Issued a statement of praise. Had a patina of perfume. Traced face and asked that face be traced."

"Turn the book to the first page." Natalya said. He had almost forgotten that she was standing there beside him, so intent was he on correctly representing what had transpired. "Turn to the first page," she repeated. He did so, and saw his own name there. "I, Shuvalov," it said. She took a step toward him. Now he could feel the heat rising off her skin. "Put your fingers on your name," she said. "Touch it." He did, and she placed her hand atop his again. Desire rushed through him; he knew that any moment now, he would see the most passionate and lurid of all reds. At the last second, she grabbed the cover of *Collection, Section V* and slammed the book shut on his fingers.

Shuvalov came awake with a start. He blinked his eyes to try to recapture the red, but it was gone. Natalya was gone as well. He tried to summon up a memory of her, but every image he managed to generate was composed of pieces of other portraits: eyes from Michelangelo, mouth from Titian, smooth limbs and breasts from Cranach. The clock in the corner read half past three. He tried to collect his thoughts. His heart was beating fast, and his head was pounding. No: it was not his head. It was the door. But the noise was entirely different than the noise he had been hearing each afternoon; this was a softer thudding. "Stop," Shuvalov shouted. "Please stop." He could not pull himself to his feet for a few minutes; he was still half in his dream and half in the world, and by the time he got to the door, the noise had ceased and the hallway was empty.

~

At court, Prince Nikolai was nowhere to be found. Shuvalov hurried to the archway where he had first seen Natalya. She was not there, of course, but the place, and the way the light came in through the window, brought her back to him. Then Shuvalov felt a presence at his back. He tensed. Could this be Natalya? A hand came to rest on his shoulder. It was a heavier hand than the hand he had dreamed. "Ivan Ivanovich," a voice said. Shuvalov turned around. It was Nikolai. "I must tell you," Nikolai said, "I came to your chambers, but you did not answer the door." Shuvalov began to apologize. "No, no," said the prince. "I understand."

Shuvalov and the prince looked out the window at the garden. "Do you ever feel as though you should catalogue nature in addition to art?" the prince said. "By that, I only mean to say that nature sometimes furnishes scenes that are as perfectly composed as a painting."

"I must get back to my chambers," Shuvalov said.

"Of course," said Nikolai, his tone heavy with disappointment.

Shuvalov was halfway across the ballroom when he turned back toward the prince. "Nikolai," he said. "Would you like to accompany me to my chambers now?"

The two of them, Shuvalov in the lead, went back down the long hall toward the library. Shuvalov opened the door and the prince stepped past him into the room. Shuvalov moved to the desk, lifted the current volume of the *Collection*, turned it in his hands so that the prince could see it from every angle. Shuvalov announced that if the prince liked, he could stay while Shuvalov worked. The prince nodded eagerly and took a seat. Shuvalov moved into position behind his desk. He straightened the Arcimboldo so that it pleased him. He entered a French landscape that was attributed to Claude, and a Bible illustrated by Picard, and an Etruscan bust, doing his best to explain his method to the prince, and felt his strength returning.

II. Fun with Time

Editor's Note:

"Fun with Time," the title of this piece, was also the title of a letter that Mr. Greenman sent me years ago from Tibet: "What is lost to time? Imagine it as a romantic issue if you like—a girl whose face you loved to stare at is suddenly gone, and all you can recover is the sound of her voice. This is not precisely accurate but neither is it a total misrepresentation." This illustrates not only his horological obsessions, but his painful awareness of the folly of permanent decisions. He has always been uncomfortable with picking one literary style, because, as he has said, "the illusion of permanence is the cruellest joke around." But I shouldn't say much more. When we were first working on *Superworse*, and I was beginning to sketch out some rudimentary annotation, he sent me a note that said, "Your annotations will be longer than the pieces they are attached to." I have taken great pains to ensure that this is not the case.

Obtain a watch without fluorescent-tipped hands. Go into a pitch-black room. Hold the watch to your ear. Then close your eyes. Is the ticking any louder?

Locate a small child who can speak but not yet tell time. Ask the child what time it is. When the child answers, believe him.

Find an ordinary kitchen timer and set it for three minutes. At the conclusion of the three minutes, divorce your wife or husband. If you are not married, marry the first available person, reset the timer, and repeat the exercise.

Each time the minute hand overlaps the hour hand, pretend that the hour hand has disappeared. As quickly as possible, work yourself into a panic imagining a world with no hours, only minutes. The next time you feel happy, look at a clock and note how long it takes until you are miserable.

When a friend asks you what time it is, say, "Time to take off my watch and put it in my pocket." Then take off your watch and put it in your pocket.

I. WHAT 100 PEOPLE, REAL AND FAKE, BELIEVE ABOUT DOLORES

Editor's Note:

For me, this final chapter is an anticlimax, but perhaps I should set aside my own reaction, for at least two critics have singled it out as the apogee of Mr. Greenman's work. These fawning assessments do not strike me as particularly true, but as I have said, I am a somewhat harsh critic of Mr. Greenman's work, and maybe my reaction to it is not representative. I should also mention that the heterotopic trope used here, in which real and unreal people interact, was first suggested by Mr. Greenman in a class of mine he took more than a decade ago, and that, in an attempt to credit me with my role in developing this idea, he penned an early draft of this story in which I was among the hundred characters. But he had in mind a specific ratio between the real and the unreal, so I was deleted.

Ruth, her friend: That she never meant to hurt Tom.

Arthur, Tom's brother: That if she never meant to hurt Tom, then she probably wouldn't have done the things she did.

Max, Tom's friend: That she was young and immature and that she was on the outs with Tom almost from the minute they started dating.

Hal, Tom's friend: That she was almost as tall as Tom.

Anne, her mother: That she was a young woman who always wanted certain things from life. That a husband was one of them.

That when she said a husband, she meant someone wealthy, not a millionaire necessarily, but someone with a stable job. That she wanted someone who wasn't her father.

Lou, her father: That she was a beautiful girl, and that he was sorry that he left when he did, and that over the last twenty years he thought about her often.

Sigmund Freud: That she had issues with her father's abandonment, and that it was a major contributor to her romantic pattern.

Superman: That the underwear she wore was the same as the underwear that Lois Lane wore.

Heather, her childhood friend: That she was beautiful when she was young.

June, her college roommate: That she was beautiful when she was young.

Gina, her college roommate: That she thought she was beautiful, and that she worried about it all the time.

Paul, her former boyfriend: That she was beautiful when she didn't worry too much about being beautiful. That she was different from her mother and her sister, darker, a little more dangerous.

Modigliani: That she was a woman he might have painted, and did, many times.

Don Quixote: That she was a beautiful princess, almost as beautiful as Dulcinea.

Keith, her college friend: That she liked to say that she was imprisoned in a man's body, with a man's mind and a man's eye.

Frank, her college friend: That when she joked about being a gay man, she wasn't joking entirely. That when they met, they were both sophomores, and he was out, very out, flamboyantly so, and she came right up to him after class and said, "I know all about you," and he said, "I'm sorry," very archly, and she said, "I know all about you because I am just like you." That they were friends from then on.

Leila, her younger sister: That she spent too much time on the telephone, and was bossy, but that when she went away to college the house was too quiet.

Nancy, her former boss: That she worked in an ice-cream shop during high school as a scooper, and that there was some money missing from the register during her shift. That when she was confronted, she swore that she had nothing to do with it and didn't know a thing about it. That she seemed too nervous and defiant for someone who didn't know a thing about it.

Dick Tracy: That she did not do her part in fighting crime.

Kim, her college friend: That she didn't know what she wanted to do after graduation. That she stumbled into politics because that's what Kevin was doing.

Isabel, her college friend: That Kevin was her first great love.

Kevin, her former boyfriend: That she didn't have an easy time with things, that she would cry sometimes for no good reason, that she ground her teeth when she slept. That she was ashamed of this sadness, and furious that it appeared sometimes in the office, or in the car. That once, when he caught her crying in the shower and reached out to touch her shoulder, she blinked her sorrow away, just closed her eyes and when she opened them was disconcertingly serene. That she said "what," and though he had come to console her he found himself suddenly overmastered.

That it was as if he were the patient and she the doctor. That he felt a bit humiliated, and murmured an apology, and slunk out of the bathroom. That she emerged later to continue her interrogation, and asked if he considered her an object of pity. That he said of course not. That she scowled, and then smirked. That when she left three weeks later, and it came as a complete surprise, he should have known what she meant when she said that men were always more blind than women.

George, her former boyfriend: That she said she had never loved Kevin. That she said that she had never been in love at all. That she said that it was about sex, mostly, and friendship, a little bit. That she wanted to stay in politics but wanted to work for a different campaign. That introducing her to Jim was a mistake, because Jim introduced her to Tom.

Jim, her co-worker: That she was the right woman for the job. That the campaign needed a good press assistant, someone who was personable and pretty but could also smell blood and go in for the kill. That she was a great friend, for a while.

Maurice, her co-worker: That she brightened up the place.

Demetria, her co-worker: That she was fun in elevators. That it's a strange thing to remember, but very vivid: once in an elevator, she pretended that the car had stopped between floors and made up an elaborate story about what would happen, the rescue, the injuries. That this was apparently not the only time she had done this.

Hannah, her co-worker: That it was love at first sight for her and Tom. That you could almost see a little arc of electricity between them. That if Tom hadn't been Jim's cousin, she would have run off with him right then and there. That she restrained herself out of friendship for Jim, although it's not anything she would admit. That when she found out that Jim and Tom didn't get along all that well, she called Tom herself and asked him out to dinner.

Captain Ahab: That he would have liked to meet her.

Wendy, Tom's mother: That she was good for Tom. That she was tough, but Tom needed some toughening up, since if he was left to his own devices he would have just kept on with his novel, or his play, or whatever it was he was writing that day.

Bruce, Tom's father: That she reminded him of his wife.

Seth, Tom's younger brother: That she was cool. That after she and Tom moved in together, she used to have great parties and invite all the younger kids and not make a big deal about drinking or anything. That she was hot, too.

Howard Atkin, waiter: That she and Tom tipped well.

Oscar Johnson: That she wasn't one of those people who looked at you funny if you were down on your luck. That she gave money to you if you asked for it.

Randy, Tom's friend: That she wasn't so helpful. That when she and Tom got the apartment, a bunch of friends went over to give them a hand. That she said she was supervising.

Tom Sawyer: That she would not have painted the fence.

Jennifer Antone, psychologist: That she and Tom moved in together too quickly. That she had unresolved parts of her personality that were clearly not going to resolve without some hard work. That she was uncertain about her career choice, and a little resentful that so much of the work fell to her with so little of the credit. That she had discovered something about the senator. Frida, her friend: That she had discovered something about the senator, or that at the very least her attitude toward him changed.

That he had been a kind of father figure to her at first, but that after a while he was someone she didn't quite trust.

Leo, her co-worker: That she started to put in longer hours after the first six months. That usually she wasn't the only one there late. That Demetria or Jim would stay, too. That she would call Tom and tell him that she wouldn't be home until late. That she would say, "Don't wait up," like it was a line she heard from a movie.

Senator Charles Gowdy: That she was an excellent employee, both during the campaign and after the election, never late to work, never in a bad mood, always curious, always pleasant.

Sammy Glick: That she was kissing ass to get ahead.

Janice, her grandmother: That an old woman shouldn't say bad things about a young woman, and a grandmother especially shouldn't say bad things about her granddaughter, but that there was something off about her. That maybe it's not so bad to criticize if what you're criticizing is something you recognize in yourself. That there was a woman once who worked for Senator Lyndon Johnson some forty years earlier, and that this woman had a dalliance with Senator Johnson that lasted a few months and took place mostly in hotels and limousines. That this woman had no regrets, and that her granddaughter was cut from the same cloth. That the young woman liked for a time to pretend that the senator had disappointed her as a way of putting distance between the two of them, but that the spark in her eyes gave her away.

Lyndon B. Johnson: That if that girl didn't fuck that senator, politics ain't what it used to be.

Doris, Tom's grandmother: That she had a man who loved her, and that she made him sad. That it would have been nosy to ask more. That Tom came down to Florida and moped like he was still fourteen years old and sweet on his first crush.

Ralph Kramden: That she should have been sent to the moon.

Luciana, her friend: That she and Tom hit a bump and that it made her really angry. That she said that he should have trusted her instead of running away. That she said that things would work out, one way or another, with or without Tom. That she laughed when she said it like she didn't quite believe it.

Cindy, Tom's friend: That she might have been fooling around with a girl, or at least Tom thought so.

Arthur Morris, bus driver: That she wore a skirt one time that was cut up the side so high that you could see right clear to her parts.

T-2: That she knew that violence was no solution.

Julie, neighbor: That when she moved into the apartment building, she and Tom were going through a rough patch. That he had accused her of seeing someone else behind his back, and she had admitted it, and they were separating for a few months to see how things felt. That she was upset enough by this to talk about it to a total stranger in the elevator on her first day in the building.

Warren, neighbor: That she worked terribly late hours. That she traveled on weekends, sometimes with the senator. That after about six months in that new building, she moved out. That she had reconciled with her boyfriend and was moving back in with him. That she was going to cut back her work hours and try to live a more normal life. That that's what she said, "more normal life." That she was excited enough about this to talk about it to a total stranger late at night in the lobby of the building.

Pauline, friend: That although she thought that Tom would take her back with no conditions, he was pretty angry and had in fact already moved on a little bit, that he had been with other women and thought about life without her, and that the things he wanted from her were at that point demanded rather than asked.

Peter, her second cousin: That he hadn't seen her since she was a little kid, when her father used to take her around from bar to bar. That she sat down on a stool and ordered a beer and then announced who she was. That she looked terrible, not just exhausted but distracted, and that she said that she had just moved back in with her boyfriend, which was good, but that he had kicked her out for the night, which was bad.

Pvt. Carl Radizio: That when he met her in a bar downtown, she was drunk, because that's the only reason she would have called him "Honey" from the start. Also, that she was still drunk later that night, when she went home with him and told him that she had always had a fantasy about soldiers.

Uncle Sam: That she was good for morale.

Andy Warhol: That she could have been even more fantastic.

Trisha, her childhood friend: That she would become a famous singer, because that's what she always said she wanted to be.

Jack, high school music teacher: That she was extraordinarily gifted.

Paul, college music teacher: That she had been told, somewhere along the way, that she was extraordinarily gifted, and that it got in the way of actual development of her talent, which was considerable.

Billie Holiday: That she could get inside a song and live there.

Lorraine, her friend: That she had some trouble being faithful. That she was seeing this guy Jay at the same time that she was seeing Kevin, and that she said that they wouldn't find out because she was so different with the two of them that they probably thought they were seeing different girls. That she was sad with Kevin and kept herself feeling small. That she was happy with Jay, and sang all the time.

Jay, former boyfriend: That she had a beautiful voice. That she used to sing in the shower, amazing old jazz songs. That she said that she would rather sing in the shower than have sex in the shower, but that she did both.

Gervaise, friend: That she said she wasn't planning on voting for the senator when he came up for reelection. That she laughed and said that she hadn't voted for him the first time. That she laughed again and said that she had never voted at all.

Elizabeth Cady Stanton: That she squandered her hard-fought right to vote.

Paolo, Tom's friend: That she was bad for him, because when they were apart, he suddenly started to produce work. That in three years with her, he had managed to write only a handful of stories, but that without her he wrote hundreds of pages in three months. That it was much better than the things he had written with her.

Martine, former college professor: That she had trouble growing up. That it was easy to keep an eye on her, since she was usually the one who filled up a room. That she went from high school to college on this wave of achievement and ambition, and that she hit a kind of wall where boys became as important to her as anything else. That after college, she wrote letters, and those letters were mostly about small rips and tears in her identity, until she met Tom, and then the letters were about being happy, which was for her a rarity.

Dracula: That she had a lovely neck.

Virginia Andrews, psychologist: That she was conflicted about her sexual identity, which is not particularly surprising, since most people are to some degree, but that she was unusually articulate about it. That she was not faithful to Tom and had not been faithful to Tom since the beginning of their relationship, that in fact she saw her time with Tom was itself a kind of infidelity to a previous boyfriend, and so on and so on. That she viewed herself as a gay man, and said so several times, and drew parallels between herself and her gay male friends, such as a certain promiscuity, a certain secrecy, a certain defensiveness. That her relationship with her father was almost certainly at the root of these problems.

Margaret Brel, psychologist: That she switched therapists when they told her things she didn't want to hear, which is a dangerous practice. That she had been seeing Jennifer Antone, who is a wonderful psychologist, until Jennifer told her that she needed to deal with her feelings about her father. That she moved on to Ginny Andrews, and that didn't seem to work out, and she left for Don Rogers, who is not much of an analyst but has a wonderfully comforting manner, and that evidently even Don was too confrontational for her. That she used to fight Don on even the simplest recommendation. That he eventually said, "Why don't you go see Dr. Brel?"

Don Rogers, psychologist: That she was extremely seductive. That patients had been seductive before, sometimes even attractive female patients, but that she had a certain determination that made it problematic to keep her as a patient.

Mary Poppins: That she was always complicating things that were really quite simple.

Elisabeth, Tom's sister: That she and Tom both seemed frustrated after they moved back in with each other.

Janice, Tom's former girlfriend: That she was friendly enough, even though she knew that Tom hadn't exactly been by himself during the time they were separated. That she said that she wanted to be very clear about her relationship with him,

Elaine, Tom's friend: That she was genuinely happy when Tom found a publisher for his book.

Trudy, co-worker: That she wanted to leave the senator's office. That she wasn't hiding it, so much, because that was one of the first things she said when you met her. That her boyfriend had just sold a book, and that his agent thought it might be a great screenplay.

Patrice, neighbor: That she and Tom were the guests of honor at a party that a friend was giving for Tom. That she was nervous about it because she hadn't seen lots of his friends since before the first time they broke up.

Jackie, Tom's friend: That she was so thankful that she didn't have to have the party at her house. That she said she was a horrible hostess. That she helped plan, though, and helped make the food. That she felt like things were looking up for her and Tom, and that the time apart had been a great help.

Doug, party guest: That she drank too much too early and started talking about how she hadn't really ever known her father.

Marcus, Tom's agent: That she got completely drunk and went around telling everyone that Tom's book was about her. That Tom's book was in fact about a young athlete, a runner, who ripped up his right leg in a car accident and then embarked on a career as an artist. That when someone asked her about this she admitted that she hadn't read Tom's book and wandered off to get another drink.

Ariana, party guest: That she got completely drunk and started hitting on everyone there. That it didn't matter if they were men or women. That she kissed a woman out on the patio.

Jane, party guest: That they had a fight, she and Tom.

Kimberly, party guest: That they had a fight, she and Tom.

Robin Hood: That they had a fight, she and Tom.

Calvin Coolidge: That they had a fight, she and Tom.

Paula, party guest: That they had a fight, she and Tom, and that by the end she was screaming.

Luke Skywalker: That she left the party without Tom.

Yolanda, neighbor: That she came home from the party without Tom.

Marcel Duchamp: That she turned on the television and sunk into a chair.

Mariel Hemingway: That she poured herself a drink, and then poured herself another drink.

Aristotle: That she expected that Tom would come through the door at one, or two, but that he didn't.

Marvin Gaye: That she expected that Tom would come through the door at three, or four, but he didn't.

Betsy Ross: That she expected that Tom would at least call her, but he didn't.

Paul McCartney: That she kept watching television.

Jay Gatsby: That she turned on both televisions, the one in the bedroom and the one in the living room.

Popeye: That she sat between them. That the blue glow of the TV sets sank into her until it became indistinguishable from her very being.

Lucy Ricardo: That if you're on television every night, you're poured into so many homes that you can hardly keep track of them. That now and again you pick up a signal from one place or another, and you pay closer attention. That if a baby is being born in a house with the set on, you can sense that. That you can also sense suicides. That one night, during the episode with the blacked-out teeth, she started staring straight ahead. That her eyes were open, but that she didn't laugh or cry or anything, just stared. That it was as if she was gone out of her body. That she was like that for more than twenty minutes. That when she finally got up to change the channel it was a relief, because whatever happened to her after that couldn't have been good.

Tracy, Tom's friend: That Tom came over and slept on the floor. That Tom was drunk and Tom was angry. That Tom said it was over between the two of them.

Lt. Oswaldo Sepulveda: That she placed a call to the precinct saying that someone had tampered with the locks on her front door.

Lt. Columbo: That there was something suspicious about the way that Tom's car was parked outside Tracy's apartment. That there was also something suspicious about the fact that there were no signs of tampering on the front door lock. That there was something suspicious about the fact that her phone was off the hook, and that his car battery was dead.

Tom: That he never meant to hurt her.

AFTERWORD
by Laurence Onge

I am dying. It is not melodramatic to say this if it is true. It is a simple fact, a kind of weather report. It is always the truest thing a man can say and yet it is the proximity of the event that we are indicating when we speak. For me, the boat is sailing. The appendix is in place. The stars are all hung in the sky, and if they are now just beginning to melt, that is a shame, but not a surprise.

I am not dying. I am as healthy as a horse: a sickly horse, admittedly, one that mostly just stands by the fence and watches traffic, but not yet a dying horse. In a book so full of fictions, can I not attempt one of my own? It is exhausting and even galling to be confined to the world of that which is. That world is for natural phenomena, for the stones that sit at the bottom of a riverbed, for the river that cuts through the countryside, for the sea that refuses no river. It is not for men.

Throughout Superworse, *I have tried to act as a teacher, counselor, and confessor for Mr. Greenman. Sometimes this has been done without his consent. But, I have persevered, because I believe that my guidance is vital to his survival.*

There is a story I wish to tell that may illuminate my belief:

There was a boy. He was a sensitive boy with glasses. One day he noticed that a lightbulb was out, and he decided to climb up a ladder to change it. Near the top rung, the lightbulb suddenly, glaringly, came to life. The boy was startled, and he fell backwards, landing on a pile of books and papers, and while he was not hurt, his pride could not be repaired: not that day, not

151

the next, and not even years later. Who turned on the light? Who deceived the boy into believing that the bulb was dead in the first place? His father. This echoes the Icarus myth—it is a story of flight and light, and the sun, and the fight between father and son—and it can be read as a tale about my relationship with my own father, who was a rather rough-and-tumble man who did not take well to my literary predilections. It can also be read as a comment on my relationship with Mr. Greenman—and, given what I have disclosed about this book thus far, I feel that it should. I have suddenly turned on a light, and he may feel that he is falling. I urge him to take the fall. Shakespeare puts it best: "Thou Icarus; thy life to me is sweet. If thou wilt fight, fight by thy father's side; And, commendable proved, let's die in pride." I mentioned this once to Mr. Greenman. He dismissed Icarus as "a guy who didn't use enough wax" and Shakespeare as "a guy who used too much." I have not spoken to Mr. Greenman for a number of months and yet he is in my heart more than ever.

APPENDIX: Sad and High-Kicking

by Laurence Onge

Groucho Marx once said there are two kinds of people in the world, those who divide the world into two groups and those who do not. That is apparently an example of his trademark wit—I do not know much about Mr. Marx apart from the fact that his brother was mute—but it is also the basis of so much of today's advanced scientific thought. By and large, people believe in mutually exclusive categories that condition and confine the properties of objects: for example, it is commonly accepted that a thing which is large cannot also be small, and that a thing which is living cannot also be dead. But there is another line of thought, that of complementarity, that holds that objects can participate both in a certain state and in the opposite of that state at once, can be hot and cold, off and on, contracting and expanding. Niels Bohr, the Danish physicist who investigated the wave/particle duality, spent his last years exploring this notion, and wondering whether what applies to physical phenomena might also apply to philosophy, politics, psychology, and so forth. I cannot speak to the validity of complementarity in physics and mathematics—my expertise in both fields can be summed up in the fact that I once dropped a calculator—but the extrapolation to the humanities strikes me as an idea that has been insufficiently explored in the years since Bohr. In fact, this principle can be employed to make an important point about Mr. Greenman's work, which is both serious and funny. As I have said several times in my editorial comments in this edition, the original hardback iteration of his book did not, perhaps, make this clear enough. As I have also said, I take much of the blame for this; as the book's editor, I was not evenhanded with my enthusiasm, which canted heavily toward a certain genre of comedy piece that Mr. Greenman invented: namely, celebrity musicals based on current events and the lives of prominent celebrities. I fell in love with them the way a man falls in love with another person, and I let my passion for them run positively amok. At every opportunity, I promoted those musicals at the expense of the rest of the material. I devalued the other stories and in one case actually spat upon them, one by one, in a manuscript given to me by Mr. Greenman for safekeeping. This was certainly counterproductive: as a result of what he called my "idiotic badgering and boosterism," Mr. Greenman wrote a final musical in which he vowed to stop writing musicals entirely. That piece, "Fragments from The Death of the Musical! The Musical!" spoke of an unnamed crisis facing the United States and, in retrospect, seems to precisely predict the events of September 11, 2001.

I repeat: That piece, "Fragments from The Death of the Musical! The Musical!" spoke of an unnamed crisis facing the United States and, in retrospect, seems to precisely predict the events of September 11, 2001.

If I was convinced of the genius of these pieces before the publication of "Fragments from The Death of the Musical! The Musical," I was even more convinced afterwards.

But then there were no more, and after Mr. Greenman grudgingly allowed me to share these coruscating works with the world in the hardback edition of Superbad, *he stipulated that they be removed from all future editions. I hope that here, in the pages of* Superworse: A Novel, *I have recalibrated his oeuvre and restored the rest of the pieces to their rightful place. If I have not, it is not for lack of attempting to try.*

Still, I would be something of a turncoat if I abandoned the musicals entirely. Just last week, lying in bed, I turned to my companion and said, "Pass me the cognac."

"Get it yourself," my companion said.

"Someone's acting bitchy," I said. Then I said, "I have an idea. What if I printed the musicals in an appendix? Could the Author"—for that is how I refer to him in the privacy of my own home; it is an ironic honorific—"possibly object to that? He specified that these pieces never again appear in Superbad, *but is this not* Superworse?" *My companion laughed. I laughed. Now, perhaps, with the presentation of these marvelously diverting entertainments, you can laugh as well—and also cry, for complementarity applies here as it does elsewhere. And it is with this that I return to the estimable Groucho Marx, who once said that theatrical works are either "sad or high-kicking."*

Sad and high-kicking, Mr. Marx. Sad and high-kicking.

PUBLISHER'S NOTE:

At the request of the author, all musicals have been removed from the book and now appear at www.bengreenman.com.